The Bellevue Boys

by

Bryan Cantrell

Bryan Cantrell

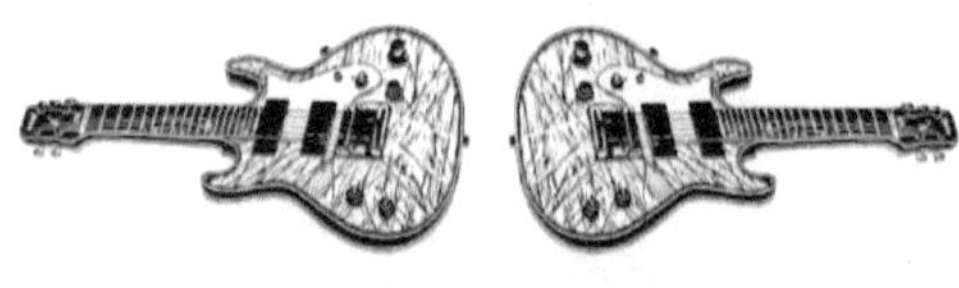

An '80s Rock 'n' Roll

Headbanging Rom-Com

The Bellevue Boys

Entertainment Production Company

The Bellevue Boys is a work of fiction. Names, characters, places, and incidents are the product of the author's imagination and are used fictitiously. The 1980s may have been the most iconic era to grow up in and some of the story might be inspired by the author's personal experiences, but the contents of this book are completely fictionalized and possibly never really happened in real life… most likely anyway. Again, for the record—fiction.

CHAPTER 1 1

CHAPTER 2 13

CHAPTER 3 23

CHAPTER 4 39

CHAPTER 5 49

CHAPTER 6 54

CHAPTER 7 74

CHAPTER 8 83

CHAPTER 9 91

CHAPTER 10 95

CHAPTER 11 118

CHAPTER 12 132

CHAPTER 13 137

CHAPTER 14 141

CHAPTER 15 155

CHAPTER 16 178

CHAPTER 17 190

CHAPTER 18 199

CHAPTER 19 205

CHAPTER 20 212

CHAPTER 21 218

CHAPTER 22 230

CHAPTER 23 253

CHAPTER 24 263

CHAPTER 25 266

CHAPTER 26 269

A LITTLE MORE ABOUT ME BEFORE YOU GO...... 273

CHAPTER 1
Rock Gods

In a time when music wasn't merely an auditory experience but a visual spectacle, emanating from the small screens perched atop dressers, desks, or even makeshift entertainment centers constructed from a board of wood resting on a stack of bricks, the youth of the day decked themselves in the attire and hairstyles of the rock deities who reigned over the airwaves of MTV.

Four hundred eighty-five miles from the hottest rock clubs of Los Angeles like the Troubadour, the Roxy and the Whisky a Go Go, Adam stood in the center of his room—the inner sanctuary of an eighteen-year-old high school graduate surrounded by posters of his favorite bands. Those images of the spandex-clad, long-haired, eyeliner-wearing hairbands were intermixed with the hottest supermodels on the planet—Christie Brinkley and Cindy Crawford ranked high holding prominent positions alongside Mötley Crüe, Ratt and Van Halen.

Adam adjusted the leather strap of his glossy black Fender Stratocaster that contrasted beautifully with its white inlaid pickguard. He moved his long wavy black hair to dislodge it from its position, trapped under the strap against his shoulder. He checked himself out in the mirrored closet door. Cool.

Jessica looked up at him from her seat on the queen-sized waterbed. They had been dating for almost a year now, and it had been mostly great. He had just graduated from high school, while she had one more year to go. He was short, but still a good four inches taller than her, handsome, and mildly popular. He was the kind of guy whose great qualities you'd notice once you got to know him, but he wouldn't stand out at a party. An acquired taste. The best part about that was that she didn't have to worry about a bunch of skanks hitting on him when she wasn't around.

Everything had been going great until he graduated. Now, he was just annoying her daily. He planned on leaving for Northern Arizona University at the end of summer, assuming that she'd just wait around for him. More irritating was that he was more worried about being far away from his friends and bandmates than leaving her behind.

She glanced at the project he had promised to help her with but had done exactly squat for. Beside her were a photo album and several stacks of photos. She narrowed her eyes, heavily lined with black liner and blue shadow, as she looked up at her self-absorbed boyfriend.

"Jess, check this out," he said.

Adam held the guitar in front of him and counted to three, then sent it flipping all the way around his body to arrive back at the playing position. He double-lifted his brows proudly at her and waited for her approval of his theatric performance.

"How cool would that look on stage?"

"So cool. How are you going to do that when it's plugged in?" she asked with a generous helping of sarcasm.

Adam leaned down and picked up the guitar cord and plugged it into the Strat. He looked down at the length of the long cord attached to a small amplifier sitting on a shelf crowded with stacks of cassette tapes. He then pulled a bit of the cord toward him to create some slack then sailed his guitar around his back again. CRASH—the amp was yanked off the shelf, knocking dozens of cassettes to the floor along with it.

"Shit."

"Oh my God. I don't know how someone so smart can be such an idiot. You were going to help me with this photo album from prom. Can you quit playing with your stupid guitar?"

Adam started to pick up the mess he had just made.

"Sorry, but me and the boys are gonna have band practice, I just need to work on some new tricks."

"You could practice playing, that would be a good trick."

"I was practicing… before you got here."

"Fine. Can you help me choose what else to put in our prom album?" Jessica continued to organize the photos arranged on the bed.

Adam set the guitar down and picked up some of the

photos. He started to sort through the collection of prom pictures. He thumbed through the shots of dancing, images of the two of them dressed up in a tuxedo and gown, then he found a photo of himself and three other boys with long hair standing together with cigarettes hanging from their lips.

"You've got to have a page of me and the boys. This one is so cool," Adam said handing her the photo.

"I don't want a whole page of just you and your stupid friends in my album."

"Okay, okay, I get it."

Adam, a little hurt, wandered over to his desk and started looking through cassette tapes that were stored in a rack. He was not so much interested in the music as just wanting to avoid going through the prom memories with Jessica.

"Maybe you should make an album to take with you to college. That way when you're missing me you can look through it," Jessica said hopefully.

"Hmm? Oh, it's cool. I have a shoe box with all my photos." He grabbed a box from under his desk and brought it over to the bed. He looked over the spread and spotted a separate stack on its own. Adam opened the box and then he unceremoniously plopped the photos inside. "These are the doubles, right?"

Jessica stared daggers at him while he slipped the box back under the desk.

"Gods! Just shove our whole relationship into a shoe box under your desk why don't you!"

She slammed her album closed and put the photos away in her purse in a huff. Adam hurried over to her and put his arms around her.

"When I'm missing you up in the cold north of Flagstaff, I'll just call you. And I don't need a picture to remind me of how hot you are. I can just close my eyes and I see your beautiful face, your long blonde hair," Adam held her chin up to look into her hurt eyes, "those magical eyes. Besides, I'll be back for the holidays and summers."

He leaned in and started to kiss her with his eyes beginning to close but saw that Jessica was not into the moment.

"Ahem."

The two teens were startled by a woman clearing her throat loudly in the doorway. They turned to see Adam's mom, Judy, standing in the doorway dressed in a pant suit with sassy, styled-short, dyed blonde hair. Her eyes looked Jessica up and down, oozing judgement on her rocker T-shirt with the blond lead singer of the band Poison displayed on it, then her eyes moved on to her choice of skintight jeans that laced up the front like a sneaker instead of relying on a good old-fashioned zipper.

"Jessica, I didn't know you were over. You look so… fashionable today. You're so lucky that you have such a cute figure and can get away with wearing… well, jeans without zippers are- interesting." She turned to her son. "I'm taking your sister to the mall for some new shoes. We'll be gone for about an hour. Are you two eating dinner with us?"

"No, Mom. I'm working tonight."

Judy looked at Adam, then at Jessica who was still sitting on the bed, then back to Adam again. A worried thought seemed to go through her mind.

"Well, maybe you should be starting to get ready."

"I've got like almost two hours or so," said Adam dismissively.

Judy and Jessica were just about staring each other down now, eye-daggers flashing between them. Jessica put her bare feet onto the bed and lay down seductively propped up on her elbow. Her tanned midriff was now showing taut, youthful skin underneath the small T-shirt. There was a hint of a smile that emerged on her face as she saw fear creep into Judy's eyes as they widened.

"We'll go to the store later. I've got some laundry to finish." She stood in the doorway uncomfortably, then turned to go.

"Oh, Mom. Can you toss this stuff in too?" Adam handed her a small pile of clothes that was stuffed behind his door. His mom left with her arms full and Jessica smiled with a shake of her head. Adam grabbed his guitar again and continued to work on his poses in the mirror.

"Are you guys ever going to play a gig?"

"Definitely. But we're not totally ready yet. We're still working on our sound." He turned to look over his shoulder at his backside.

"You've been finding your sound for like three years now."

"I wish the boys were going to NAU with me this fall."

Jessica was watching him as he continued to change his pose. She noticed the sound of stomping feet approaching the doorway and cringed inwardly, thinking his mom was marching her way back.

Adam's sister Mandy showed up in a cloud of dark curly hair and early teen angst. She was short like Adam but with an enormous presence and attitude unusual for someone who had only just finished their freshman year.

"Thanks a lot, Adam!"

"What?"

"Mom doesn't want to leave the two of you alone in the house, so I can't go to the mall."

"Why?"

"Why?" Mandy shot Jessica a look. "Because you guys will start to do the wild thing as soon as we leave."

"Oh my God!" exclaimed Jessica.

"No, we won't. We were just putting photos in an album."

"Whatever. Now I'm stuck here until *you* leave," she said with a finger pointed at Jessica, "or *you* go to work," she voiced as she turned back at Adam.

"Fine. I'm gonna go." Jessica slipped on her shoes

and gathered up her stuff to leave.

"No, Jess, wait. Don't go."

Jessica brushed past Mandy and out the bedroom door with Adam following her.

Adam started to plead with her as she rounded the hallway toward the front door. "Come on, Jess…"

Jessica stopped at the door and spun around to face Adam.

"I told you your mom doesn't like me," she started at him in a whispered shout. "It's obvious now that she thinks I'm some sort of slut."

"No, you're being too sensitive. I'm sure she likes you. She just doesn't want to be a grandma is all."

"What about that crack about my outfit?"

Adam rolled his eyes. "They wore like poodle skirts or some shit when she was our age. She just doesn't understand your fashion sense."

Mandy and Judy were in the living room standing at the corner to the hallway listening to Adam and Jessica's conversation by the front door. They quietly whispered to each other.

"Fashion sense? Try lack thereof," quipped Mandy.

"Shh," Judy said.

Jessica stood with her hand on her hips as Adam tried his best to smooth things over.

"She's always harping on what I wear too. Moms are just old-fashioned and out of touch."

"Well, she's not *my* mom."

"Thank God for that," said Judy quietly to Mandy as they continued eavesdropping.

"Shh," shushed Mandy.

"Don't be mad," Adam said with a head tilt, trying his best to be endearing.

Jessica opened the front door and walked out. Adam stood holding the edge of the open door, watching her walk down the steps toward her Volkswagen Rabbit parked on the street.

"I'm going home," she said without so much as a look back.

"I'll call you later?"

Jessica didn't answer and Adam watched her get in her car and drive away. He closed the door and moped back down the hallway to find his mom and sister standing in the living room trying their best to look like they were busy doing something besides eavesdropping.

"Thanks a lot, Mom."

"She seems pretty pissed," said Mandy.

"You don't need to get some tramp pregnant before you go to college, Adam. I'm just trying to save you a lifetime of heartache and bad decisions."

He stood there with his hands on his head, a look of annoyance on his face.

"We were just putting together a photo album. Okay, Mom?"

"I saw what you were doing. And we've had this conversation a million times. I'm not ready to be a grandma!"

"God, Mom! I'm not going to make you a grandma!" He started to huff down the hallway toward his room. "I've got to get ready for work! And maybe I don't even want to go to college!"

Judy let out a loud sigh and sat down in a chair with contained fury. She picked up a magazine from the table next to her and aggressively started to flip through its contents.

Mandy just stared at her, then looked down the hallway, then back at her mom who was ignoring her as she hovered in front, waiting on her.

"Well, do I get to go to the mall or not?" Mandy exclaimed while Judy pretended to be focused on the magazine.

CHAPTER 2
The Thorn

Adam tossed white plastic bags full of discarded popcorn and drink containers into the large metal dumpster outside the rear of the movie theater he worked at. He and his friend Ricky were closing up for the night. They both had their white button-up shirts untucked and red vests open after all the moviegoers had made it back to their cars and were headed home or on to the next form of entertainment they could find.

Adam watched the twenty-year-old, overweight Ricky struggle to keep his sand-colored moppish hair from blocking his view as he leaned over tying the ends of the trash bags before he tossed them to Adam for disposal.

"Me and Dave are meeting at the tire tree to smoke a bowl. Want to come?" asked Ricky with his signature surfer's drawl and Zen-like quality of talking.

"I'm going over to Jess's."

Ricky hefted the last trash bag to Adam to toss.

"I thought you guys were in a tiff."

"We are. Things have sucked since prom."

Adam dropped the last bag into the dumpster and removed a board of wood that was supporting the lid, sending it clanging down.

"Maybe it's because you're leaving for college at the end of summer."

"Not sure I'm going," Adam said with a sigh.

"What do you mean? I thought you were all set to go to Flagstaff?"

"I was, I am… I'm not sure Jess is going to wait for me. Plus, what will happen to my band?"

They headed back into the theater and made their

way toward the main entrance past the counters full of candy and vacant ticket booths, turning off the lights as they went.

"Dude, she is just seventeen, and a Betty, who has another year of high school left. You're cool and all but no way she's waiting for you. She's the kind of chick that's looking to date an up-'n'-coming rock star, and your band is… lacking something."

"What? What are we lacking?"

"Oh, I don't know, talent maybe."

Adam's eyes went wide at Ricky's diss. "Thanks a lot, dude. Then should I just give up on the dream and go to college? Become a doctor or a lawyer or some shit?"

Ricky pulled a key held to a retractable key ring fastened to his belt loop and locked the front glass door of the movie theater. Adam watched him finish the closing process and pulled a cigarette from his pack. He lit it with a metal lighter that had an AC/DC logo on it as Ricky turned toward him.

"Should I stay here and work on my music to keep Jessica?"

"That is the kind of shit only you can answer." Ricky pantomimed weighing with his hands. "Pursue college, pursue hot girlfriend. College, hot girlfriend."

"What would you do?"

"I walk a different path, grasshopper."

"You'd pick the hot girlfriend." Adam started heading to their cars parked next to each other.

"Well, school is stifling to a mind like mine," Ricky said with an air of authority.

"It's getting late. See you, stoner."

"Later days and better lays," said Ricky with parting wisdom.

They engaged in a hand slap and Adam got into his car and drove away.

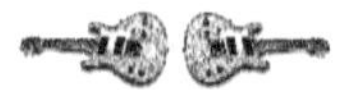

Adam cruised in his Datsun 280Z and smoked while listening to the radio. 'Every Rose Has Its Thorn' by Poison played on the radio as he made his way to Jessica's neighborhood.

We both lie silently still
In the dead of the night
Although we both lie close together
We feel miles apart inside

Was it something I said or something I did
Did my words not come out right
Though I tried not to hurt you
Though I tried
But I guess that's why they say

Every rose has its thorn
Just like every night has its dawn
Just like every cowboy sings his sad, sad song
Every rose has its thorn
Yeah it does

He downshifted into second gear and drove slowly toward her house looking for a spot on the street to park. The headlights of a parked car shined in his eyes as he approached. He squinted against the bright lights to see that the car was an orange '70s Camero with a blower sticking aggressively out of the hood. Adam caught a glimpse of a good-looking guy with long blond hair as the car passed him before the tinted window could be rolled up all the way.

"What the…? Troy?"

Adam made a U-turn and parked in the same spot as the Camero had been, right in front of Jessica's house. He quickly walked up to the door and knocked loudly. A few seconds later the door opened, and Jessica stood there, half naked, wearing only an Ozzy T-shirt that barely covered her hips. She was holding a pair of Oakley sunglasses seductively spinning them by one of their temples.

"Did you forget something?" she asked in a sing-song voice before she realized it was Adam at the door. Her face quickly dropped. "Shit."

"Yeah, Troy's sunglasses."

Adam reached out and snatched the sunglasses from Jessica's hand.

"I thought you were working. How long have you been here?"

"Long enough to see that you're cheating on me with that Axl Rose-looking poser! What the hell, Jess? How long has this been going on?"

Jessica let out a long sigh along with the truth. "Only a few weeks. And he's not a poser, Adam."

"Really? Does he play an instrument? Does he sing?

No. He just runs around in his stupid pumpkin-colored Camero dressing like he's some kind of wannabe rock star."

"You should talk," Jessica said with a head shake.

"I play guitar!"

"You suck at guitar! You've had like ten lessons, and you never practice, ever. You and your friends think your band is totally bitchin', but you bite!"

Adam took an indignant step back. "That is totally harsh! I play by ear you know."

"Whatever."

Jessica looked away from Adam for a moment, then said, "I think I want to break up."

"*You* want to break up?"

"Well, don't you?"

"Of course I want to break up! You've been cheating on me for months," yelled Adam.

"Weeks."

"Whatever." Adam started walking back to his car. "And my band doesn't suck!"

"Yeah, ya do," Jessica said quietly to herself then shut the door.

Adam came angrily through his front door and stomped down the hallway to find his dad, Lyle, his long legs stretched out in his brown La-Z-Boy recliner, wearing a Hawaiian shirt and slacks and with his cowboy boots propped up on the extended footrest, watching TV with his mom and sister. His dad greeted him without taking his eyes off the television screen.

"How was work, sport?"

"Fine," answered Adam standing there waiting to be engaged in a conversation that would allow him to vent his frustration but not wanting to start it. His dad sat there letting the sound of the show they were watching fill the silence. Adam's mom looked up at him.

"No Jessica tonight?"

"No Jessica. Ever! I broke up with her. I'm sure you're all happy as clams to hear that."

"Cause she was cheating on you?" asked Mandy.

"Did you know?" Adam asked, shocked.

"I knew she was a slut."

"We all did, dear," his mom piped in.

Adam paused and looked at his dad for confirmation. Lyle turned from the TV momentarily and gave him a look that said, *yeah, we all knew.*

"I don't want to talk about it anymore. I'm going to my room to work on my music."

He held his head high as he strode to his room with purpose.

Mandy called after him, "Tell the slut I want my Guns N' Roses cassette back!"

Adam closed the door behind him when he reached his room. He started to pace the floor, distraught and angry. His eyes landed on his Fender Stratocaster and he grabbed it, placing it forcefully on the waterbed, sending small waves back and forth across its length. He peeled off his work vest and tried to quickly take off his work shirt, but the sleeve got stuck around his wrist because he forgot to unbutton the cuff. He wrestled with it until he finally managed to rid himself of the garments that reeked of popcorn grease and cigarette smoke.

He yanked open a dresser drawer, then he swiftly shed the slacks he was wearing and slipped into a pair of leather pants. Hastily he rummaged through another drawer. He located the sleeveless Def Leppard T-shirt he was looking for and rapidly pulled it over his head. Looking at himself in the mirror, he let out a satisfied sigh of relief.

Adam picked up the guitar and put a cassette tape into his stereo. He clicked play then hurried to stand in front of the mirror again in a rock god stance. The Def Leppard song, 'Love Bites, began to play, and Adam pretended to play along, and lip-sync the words.

When you make love, do you look in the mirror?
Who do you think of, does he look like me?
Do you tell lies? And say that it's forever
Do you think twice, or just touch and see?
Ooh, babe
Oh, yeah
When you're alone, do you let go?
Are you wild and willing or is it just for show?
Ooh, come on

CHAPTER 3
I Want My MTV

The next morning Adam exited his house to find the Tucson sun shining brightly on his neighborhood. He approached his little red sports car and tentatively reached out to the metal handle anticipating it to be hot to the touch. It turned out to be not too bad. The black interior of the car was another story. He quickly rolled the windows down with the handle, and scorched his palm when he grasped the steering wheel while starting it up.

"Fuck!" Adam quickly removed his hand and shook it in hopes of cooling it down. He carefully held the wheel by the inside circle and pulled away from the curb. He slapped a Mötley Crüe cassette into the player and blasted the hard-hitting music while he drove.

One block away he turned right onto Bellevue Street and drove five houses up before he spun his car around to park beside the curb with the tires squealing. Adam exited and did a hood-slide over the slanted front end of the 280Z landing on the sidewalk. He climbed a couple of short steps to a light green-painted house, rapped on the door but didn't wait for an answer, and walked right in.

He spotted his three best friends draping themselves on the sofas and chairs watching MTV. Mark, Freddy, and Johnny glanced up at him as he found a spot to land heavily on a couch.

"S'up, homie?" asked Mark. He had long, curly dark hair and was on the heavy side for his height, which was just a little taller than Adam. The two of them had a tight bond in that they were the only two kids with Jewish heritage in their neighborhood.

"Nada. You guys?"

"Just chillin' like Dylan. Sorry to hear about you and Jess," answered Freddy with a bored tone to his voice.

"How'd you hear?" Adam looked over at Freddy's face which was a blending of his dad's Caucasian features mixed with his mom's Japanese heritage. This blending was mostly noticeable in the unique shape of his eyes and his long straight black hair. "Oh, your girlfriend, right?"

"Yeah. Jess called Cindy last night. Sorry, bro."

"She was a slut," Mark said without looking away from the TV.

"So I heard," Adam finished with a sigh.

The four boys sat without talking while a Duran Duran video finished up and the channel went to a commercial. Adam let out a louder sigh, and Johnny rolled his eyes and fidgeted his long, lanky frame in a large, cushioned chair.

"Life sucks," Adam bemoaned.

"You're not gonna be a pussy and start crying over her, are you?" Johnny asked, rubbing his face in irritation. If there was a bully in their odd group, it was him.

"No, but it still sucks."

Johnny turned to look hard at him and spout a bit of 'Johnny wisdom': "Dude, you got played. You always get played. You treat these chicks too good. Stop buying them shit and taking them on dates. *You* be the player."

"Don't listen to him. He's never even had a girlfriend," said Mark.

"Neither have you. But at least I get laid."

"I've had a girlfriend. Remember Chrissy?"

"The girl from your bar mitzvah?" asked Freddy, knowing exactly who he was talking about but setting him up for a takedown. "That was like five years ago."

"Wasn't she your cousin? "Johnny asked with a snort.

"Fuck off." Mark gave Johnny the finger.

"I can't believe she was cheating on me with Troy. Should I try to get her back?"

"You were going to have to break up with her anyway. Hello, college? NAU remember? She still has another year of high school, dude," Mark said.

"I guess. Maybe I should stay here."

"LA. That's where we need to be. All the best bands are coming out of LA," Johnny said with enthusiasm.

"We haven't even played a gig yet." Adam looked back at the TV along with the other boys. They sat in silence as a VJ talked about an upcoming concert tour. "This shit sucks. What's wrong with me? I'm starting to miss the high school days. I have no fucking clue what to do now."

Johnny's long blond hair bounced around his face while he excitedly jumped onto the couch next to Adam. "I know what you need!"

"What? Bang some other chick? Is that your answer?"

"Better! You need to take a hit from The Bad Boy," he said enthusiastically while he stood on the sofa cushions looking down at Adam.

"Ahh, great," said Mark with heavy sarcasm as Johnny ran off to his room.

"What is The Bad Boy?"

"His new bong," answered Mark.

"These dweebs won't smoke with me, but I know you can appreciate awesomeness," Johnny yelled from his room.

"Wait 'til you see this thing," Freddy said with a chuckle.

"Meet the newest member of the band. The Bad Boy." Johnny came back into the living room holding a bright red, six-foot-tall bong with dragon graphics wrapped around the giant tube. He triumphantly displayed it in front of Adam who leaned forward and checked the device out. The bong was about six inches taller than him, and he stood up for a better look. Adam found a waft of marijuana scent clinging to the acrylic tube while he climbed on the couch cushions to look down at the chamber's opening.

"Jesus Christ," said Adam.

"See, Mark, The Bad Boy can even make a believer out of a Jew."

"How do you hide this thing from your parents?" asked Adam.

"His mom hasn't set foot in his room since she walked in on him jerking off to that *Penthouse* last year," Freddy laughed.

"Shit, if I had known that was all it would take, I'd have let her catch me in junior high."

"God, you're a freak," Mark said with a head shake.

Johnny's attention was caught by the TV. "Shh, shh, check it out."

He pointed to the screen where David Lee Roth's video of 'Yankee Rose' started to play. "Turn it up, Freddy!"

The boys watched the beginning lunacy of the music video until it transitioned to the stage performance of the song while David Lee Roth strutted around with ass-less pants.

"He's so hot," Johnny said, eyes transfixed to the screen.

Adam, Freddy, and Mark looked at Johnny then at each other and then busted up laughing.

"I mean the *video* is hot," Johnny corrected himself as his cheeks flushed.

"I think you mean his ass cheeks are hot," said Mark.

"Fuck off!" Johnny turned to Adam and held out a lighter. "You gonna hit this thing, pussy?"

The boys continued to laugh, and Adam took the lighter from Johnny, "Yeah, why not?"

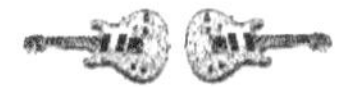

Troy checked his long blond hair in the rearview mirror and pushed a few out of place strands behind his ears. Opening the door, he slid his lanky frame out the tricked-out Camero and strode toward the front door of

Jessica's house. He was a bit hopeful that forgetting his sunglasses here last night might just end up getting him laid in the middle of the day.

He would have moved on from shagging this girl after just a few times, but something kept him coming back. Sure, she was a little hottie, but it was kind of thrilling going behind that dude Adam's back. He had known her for about a year now since she had been dating Adam, but a few weeks ago she caught him in the bathroom at a party in Freddy's house with a line of coke on the counter that he was about to partake in. She barged in without knocking and he almost shit his pants that he got caught but she shut the door behind her and asked if there was more. He was pretty low on powder, so he split his line with her, and they shared a snort.

Nothing happened that night—well, they did make out a bit in Freddy's garage while Adam and the rest of them were in the backyard drinking. Now he was having a hard time moving on. He kept thinking about her day and night. Maybe she'd dump Adam and they could start mackin' in the open.

He rapped on the front door and leaned against the house real casual and cool like, waiting for her to answer. He couldn't wait to see her welcoming smile.

The door opened and she stood there in tank top and Dolphin shorts. Troy drank in her tan shapely legs and nodded his head with a hint of a smile. *Yeah, baby,* he thought to himself.

"Hey."

"Hey. What's up? My dad's home and he's being a total jerk so I can't have anyone over."

Troy's face fell with disappointment.

"It's cool, I just left my Oakleys here last night. I tried calling but your line was busy."

"Yeah, my dad hates it when it rings while he's trying to sleep so he leaves it off the hook."

"Oh, yeah?"

"I don't have your sunglasses. Adam came over last night right after you left. He knows about us."

Troy's heart started to race, and he unconsciously straightened his frame. "Major bummer. Was he pissed?"

"Uhm, duh, he had a fucking cow. Anyway, he grabbed your Oakleys and left."

"Well, you gonna get them back for me?"

"As if. Why would I want to see him again? We broke

up. Can't *you* just get them from him?"

Troy looked around the neighborhood worriedly. *Could Adam be watching them now?* "I really don't like confrontation."

"Fine. I'll do it. I'll call you later," Jessica started to close the door.

"So, are we together now?" Troy asked.

"Like a couple?"

"Totally."

Jessica looked him over as this was something she hadn't fully considered. Did she want this guy as a boyfriend? He was hot and all, but he wasn't exactly bright. He also wasn't in a band. He looked like he was in a band, but still. "All right. I'll call you later."

Troy stood there for a moment after she shut the door. He nodded his head and pursed his lips as he made his way toward his car. There was a little strut in his step that wasn't there before. He considered a hood-slide might be in order to seal his badass-ness feeling but changed his mind to prevent the scratching of his car's sick orange paint job.

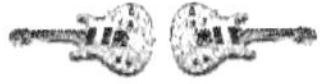

The boys were still sitting in front of the TV at Johnny's house eating from bags of chips and sipping sodas. MTV started to air the Madonna video 'Lucky Star'. Madonna was wearing tight capri leggings under her short black skirt with her midriff peeking out from her lace top as she danced and rolled around seductively.

"This song bites," Mark commented.

"So lame," agreed Adam, yet none of the boys took their eyes from the screen.

"No one is gonna remember her next year," Freddy chimed in.

"She *is* hot." Adam paused and looked over at Johnny. "No David Lee Roth though."

"Definitely not," Mark said.

"No way," Freddy agreed.

"You guys are dicks. You know I meant the video."

The boys chuckled at Johnny's expense. Freddy looked at his Swatch watch and saw the time.

"Dudes, we should really go to my house and have

band practice."

"Yeah, my mom will be home soon anyway," said Johnny.

"Let's burn some rubber, baby," Freddy said spinning his keyring around his finger that also held a bottle opener and a tiny Rubik's cube.

They turned off the TV and left their soda cans and chip bags cluttering the living room and headed out of the house. Freddy, Mark, and Adam each got into their cars parked out front and Johnny hopped on his Ninja motorcycle. Everyone unnecessarily revved up their engines before putting them into gear. Each of them peeled out of their parking spots with Freddy's car fishtailing into the middle of the street. They aggressively drove past seven houses and then pulled to a stop outside Freddy's place.

There was more revving before they turned off their engines and left their vehicles to walk up to the well-maintained single-story house.

"I got some new sticks for my drums."

"Cool, Fred, what did you get?" asked Adam.

"Black ones."

"Badass."

The boys walked into the kitchen to find Freddy's mom, Asami, and his little brother Daniel who was twelve years old and looked like a pared-down version of Freddy but with hair styled in a short bowl cut instead of the deeply black, long straight hair that Freddy meticulously groomed.

Daniel and Asami were eating noodles out of bowls with chopsticks. Asami squinted her eyes at Freddy upon seeing him bring all his friends into the house. She was tired of her elder son bringing his friends over to eat their food and drink their soda. If one of them went to her refrigerator without the politeness of asking permission she was going to get her four-foot-nine body out of this seat and smack their face like their moms should have done a long time ago.

"Mom, we're going to my room for band practice. Can you make us some snacks?"

She looked hard at her son but softened. He was such a good boy. He turned out very tall and handsome. He had a nice girlfriend, pretty and smart. If he would just cut that hair, not be so skinny and get a job she would be so proud.

"Yeah, yeah, but you need be done b'fore your dad

come home," she said in Japanese-accented English.

"Thanks, Mrs. T," said Adam.

"Thanks, Mrs. T," Johnny and Mark said in unison.

"All right, Bellevue Boys, let's rock!" Adam said with a high five to the boys that they all joined in on.

"That band name is stupid," said Daniel.

"Shut up, Daniel," retorted Freddy.

"It's where we live, man. Bellevue, The Bellevue Boys. Like we're a street gang," Mark said.

"Yeah, Daniel, like a crazy street gang from the Bellevue mental ward," Adam added in.

Asami looked over at Adam. "You don't live here. You live block away. On Helen Street."

"Well…"

"You should call yourselves The Bellevue Boys and Helen," Daniel said with a snort.

"That make more sense," Asami added.

Mark looked over at Adam. "We may just have to kick you out of the band."

"Find 'nother boy who live on Bellevue."

"Maybe one that can play guitar," Daniel quipped but looked quickly down as Adam gave him a threatening stare.

Freddy looked hard at his mom and little brother then nodded his head toward his room down the hall. "Come on, guys."

The boys headed down the hall a little less enthusiastically than when they arrived. Asami and Daniel gave each other a knowing look as they enjoyed making fun of Freddy's childhood friends. Asami has watched these boys grow up from their sweet-natured elementary school days to the rude, insensitive pimple-faced high school years. She still patiently waited for Freddy and the rest of them to start becoming the men they had the potential to be. *I make good fun of them until they get there*, Asami thought to herself with a smile.

Freddy's room was a crowded mess of amps, guitars, clothing, and a drum set in the corner by the window. The room has a permanent odor of dirty socks and sweat mixed with Polo cologne. Freddy stripped off his shirt revealing his lean torso as he sat behind the drums. Mark tied his long, black kinky hair into a top knot as he'd seen his idol Gene Simmons wear. He then strapped on his second-hand bass guitar and plugged the cord into the amp. Adam secured an unlit cigarette between the guitar strings close to the tuning pegs like he's seen Eddie Van Halen do. Johnny moved in close to the microphone attached to the stand. He took his position in a rock god pose.

"Let's start with some Crüe," Johnny suggested. He tipped his head down with his hand resting on the mic and nodded in unison as Freddy awkwardly spun one of his new sticks then clapped them together three times. They all started to jam.

Asami made a sour face from the kitchen as the sound of a badly played and sung version of 'Shout at the Devil' wafted from her son's room.

"Can't you make him live in a dorm when school starts?" Daniel asked loudly to be heard over the noise.

Asami held her hands to her ears in mock pain. "Why can't their parents buy lessons?"

CHAPTER 4
See Ya, Nacho

Adam and Mark were across the street from Freddy's shooting hoops in the driveway of Mark's home. The backboard was mounted just above the carport at a height that allowed an under six-foot white guy to dunk the ball on a good day. Adam out dribbled his heavyset friend but missed just about every layup.

"I wish you were going to NAU. It's gonna suck not having any friends up there."

"I'm kind of glad I didn't get in. I'd freeze my balls off in Flagstaff. I'll stick with community college then maybe transfer to UofA later."

"Not gonna go to LA with Johnny and Freddy, get a record deal?"

Mark scoffed and passed the ball to Adam. "Give me a break. We suck. Johnny is delusional and Freddy's parents would kill him if he moved to LA."

"You think we suck?" Adam turned to Mark before shooting the ball.

"I *know* we suck. We had two fans. Your girlfriend and Freddy's girlfriend. I'm sure we're down to one now."

Adam looked at his watch and made a face. "Shit. I got to get to work." He faked a pass to Mark and dribbled the ball to the end of the driveway. "Three seconds left on the clock. The Jew version of Spud Webb goes for the hook shot…" Adam threw a high hook shot missing the backboard completely, bouncing the ball off the pitched roof.

"You play basketball like you play guitar."

Adam gave Mark the finger as he got into his car.

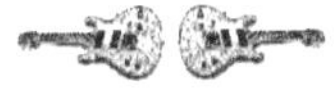

The credits rolled into the end of the movie *The Lost Boys* as Adam and Ricky were cleaning up the mess made by the moviegoers that just left the auditorium. The theater's walls were ornately decorated with faux-Roman carvings. The maroon-colored cushioned seats would recline and rock slightly by design. The enormous matching drapes that hung next to the screen would open when the movie started and close after the credits ended. The floor, sticky with soda, retained its grip on the spilt popcorn and candy that Adam tried to sweep up with his broom and dustpan attached to a stick. Ricky moved through the isle picking up soda cups, candy boxes and other discarded treats from the concession.

"Dude, if you're really not gonna go away to college than let's be Lost Boys for Halloween."

"What?"

"You, me, Freddy, Johnny, and Mark roll up to a party as cool teenage vampires. That would be bitchin'. Chicks love vampires. The hunger, the thirst, the danger. It's a seduction thing," Ricky explained.

"A seduction thing? Have you been reading your mom's Harlequin novels?"

"I *know* women. Two older sisters, a mom and an aunt gabbing at me all the time. You learn shit. Trust me."

Adam resumed his sweeping as they got closer to finishing their cleaning job. "As much as I think your idea is rad, I'll be in college getting an education. Though, if I did join you as a Lost Boy, I would be Michael."

"Whatever. Today you say you're leaving but you'll probably fall in love and wind up being my sidekick as I portray the Lost Boy vampire… Michael."

Ricky picked up a half-eaten container of nachos and started to snack on them as they walked toward the entrance of the auditorium.

"No more love for me, buddy. Jessica broke my heart, and I'm done with Tucson."

The boys opened the doors to a small crowd of people waiting to go in. Adam stopped in his tracks at the sight of a pretty girl with brown feathered hair standing in front applying lipstick with the help of a small compact mirror. Ricky bumped into Adam's back, tipping the nacho tray to spill a small helping of cheese on the back of Adam's shirt.

Adam recognized the girl immediately and was

frozen as to his next move. Tracy was her name and they'd known each other since they were little kids. Adam always had a crush on her, but she was out of his league, always dating older guys, bigger, studlier than he would ever be. *Should I keep my head down and just quickly pass before she notices me?* ran through his mind.

"Dude?" asked Ricky who was standing behind Adam wondering if he should say something about the yellow spooge that was dripping down the back of his shirt.

Tracy looked up and she and Adam made eye contact. Her face lit up and she smiled widely as she approached him, socking him affectionately on the arm.

"Hey, Adam."

"Tracy, hi. What are you doing here?"

"Um duh, seeing a movie, weirdo," she said playfully.

Ricky moved beside Adam, bumping him a bit to the side.

"What's up, Tracy? Haven't seen you in a while. You still seeing Joey?" Ricky asked with a voice about two octaves lower than his normal voice.

"He's just getting popcorn." Tracy looked at Ricky with his puffed-up chest and noticed a giant glob of nacho cheese clinging to his cheek.

"Cool. Joey and I had some of the same classes, graduated a year before you two. Barely. Well, me barely, Joey I'm sure had no problem. He seems bright."

Tracy was looking at Ricky, not wanting to focus on the cheese splotch, and unsure if she should alert him. An awkward silence just hung over the three of them. Finally, Adam edged Ricky aside.

"Anyway, it's good to see you. You're going to love the movie. Tell Joey hey."

Tracy stopped him before he went. "Adam, I wanted to say thanks for getting me through science and math classes. I don't know if I could have done it without your help."

"Oh, well, I'm sure you would have been fine. You're really smart, Trace."

"I don't know about that, but I did get into ASU."

"That is awesome! Congrats," Adam told her with a genuine smile.

"Yes, awesome. Adam here is going to NAU," Ricky added.

"Are you? I like that place. So cold in the winter though…"

"Well, I'm still not sure…" Adam started to say.

"Oh, our little buddy here will be okay up north. The cold weather will keep him focused on his education." Ricky put his hands on Adam's shoulders. "He'll probably be a proctologist or something like that."

Tracy's boyfriend Joey walked up to them holding a tub of popcorn and a drink cup. The guy was good looking in a tough, bad boy way. He was wearing jeans with stylish rips on the legs along with a tight black T-shirt stretched against a muscular chest. His eyes were in a perpetual squint and shoulder length, dirty blond hair fell around those narrowed eyes.

"I thought you were going to get us some seats?"

Tracy turned to see Joey next to her. "I ran into Adam and Ricky. We were just…"

"Whatever. Let's find a spot. I don't want to have to sit in the front row."

Ricky stepped up to attempt engaging Joey in a high five. "How's it hanging, Joey? Long time, no see, brother."

Joey pulled back, his face displaying mock horror at the glob of cheese plastered to Ricky's face. "Hey, nacho. Good to see you haven't changed much. Come on, Tracy."

Joey brushed past Adam, spilling some popcorn on the ground. He pulled Tracy along, commenting over his shoulder, "You janitors missed a spot."

Ricky and Adam watched as the pair disappeared through the doorway of the theater.

"God, that guy is such a dick," Adam said.

"One of the biggest."

"Do you think there was a vibe between me and

Tracy?"

"Totally. Like the vibe you get from an annoying dog that keeps jumping up on your leg for attention. Settle down now, Benji, the pretty girl is gone." Ricky ruffled Adam's hair like he was a poodle. Adam brushed his hand off his head.

"I've had the hots for her since sixth grade."

"Well, now that you've finally reached the height of a sixth grader maybe you have a shot," Ricky turned to look down at Adam, "not."

"You've got a little something on your face, nacho," Adam said, then raised his brows and walked away.

Joey and Tracy found a set of seats and settled in. Joey set his drink and popcorn down and checked out the crowd in the theater. He could feel the heat of Tracy's anger radiating off her as she sat quietly next to him. He knew a complaint was coming, it was just a matter of when. To further annoy her he began to toss popcorn up in the air and catch it in his mouth.

"I don't know why you have to be such an ass."

"I don't know why you want to talk to those dorks."

"Adam is a friend of mine. I've known him since elementary school, and he helped me through math."

"So, I have him to thank for your leaving to ASU. He's a dick," Joey said brushing his hair back from his eyes.

"I'm going to ASU because I want to do something with my life. Why don't you come? It's not too late. There are way more jobs in Phoenix than here."

Joey shook his head. "My mom needs me here. She can't run the car wash without me."

"I'm sure she can manage."

They sat in silence for a moment.

"I can't stay here. You know that. I need to get out of this town, Joey." She turned to look at him. "I need to get away from my mom."

Joey didn't say anything. He didn't look at her even though he knew she wanted him to. He could feel her stare against his cheek, waiting. He just watched the screen… that had nothing projected on it. He popped a few more popcorns into his mouth.

"Guess there's nothing more to say," she said with sarcasm and turned her eyes to the movie screen and prayed for the damn movie to start.

CHAPTER 5
Skank

Adam arrived home after his shift at the theater was over. He peeled off his work vest and headed down the hallway. He could hear the TV on and when he got to the living room, he saw that his mom and dad were sitting and watching a show. Adam flopped down in a chair near his mom.

"Hi, sport. How was work?" his dad asked.

"Fine. Did anyone call for me?"

"Like who? Your ex, Jessica?" his mom asked.

"Can we just say that we are so happy that's over. It is over, isn't it?" his dad piped in, hopeful.

"Yes, it's over."

"Your father and I were worried that you were going to change your mind about going away to college, so that you could stay here with the little Aqua Net queen."

Adam took a big breath. "About college, I was thinking NAU might not be the best place…"

His dad cut him off. "Adam, we've talked about this. You need to get away from your friends. Focus on your education. Being up there on your own will help you become a man, give you some confidence and get you in the right crowd."

"You can't spend the next couple of years running around aimlessly with a group of drugged-out losers," his mom added.

"They're not losers! I just, I just don't know if I want to go all the way to NAU. Maybe I can go to ASU, or maybe just stay here and go to college."

His sister, Mandy, had heard all of this from her room, and she came stomping in. "You have to go away to NAU! Mom and Dad said I can change your room into an art studio. Don't ruin your life over some sleazebag dumping you!"

"I'm not ruining my life! I just don't know what to do with it." Adam got up in a huff and left and headed to his room, then slammed the door behind him.

Mandy turned toward her parents. "You guys can't let him stay here with his idiot friends. You have to make him go away to college."

"He's an adult now. We can't force him," Lyle said with a shoulder shrug.

"Of course you can. You're the parents! One of you needs to talk to him."

Lyle and Judy both looked at each other uncomfortably, neither volunteering to do the parenting job. Mandy stood in front of them waiting, tapping a foot with impatience.

"Seems like a male perspective would be best in this situation," said Judy finally.

Lyle looked at the TV. "I'm gonna miss *MacGyver*."

"Lyle!"

"All right, I'm going." He got up with a heartbroken look toward the TV and walked down the hallway to Adam's room. He rapped his knuckles on the door before he opened it and stuck his head in. Adam was sitting on the edge of his waterbed plucking at his guitar.

"You're busy practicing. I can come back," Lyle said with maybe just a hint of hopefulness.

"No, it's cool. I'm just messing around."

Lyle came in and awkwardly sat on the bed next to him. He looked around at all the immature teen and childish decorations that coated his son's room. There was not one scrap of sports memorabilia or athletic-leaning items in the entire room. He held back a sigh that almost escaped.

"So, are you doing okay with the whole breakup thing?"

"I don't know. It sucks. I've never been cheated on before. I feel like I've been punched in the gut. And I know the guy, we've hung out."

"Yeah, it's a raw deal," Lyle said trying to use a bit of youthful slang.

"And I miss her. We've been together almost a year. Then she cheats on me with that dweeb…" Adam was visibly upset. He got up from the waterbed with his guitar and sat in his desk chair. The bed sloshed and Lyle rode the wave of the bed as it settled. He was unsure of what to say to his son.

"Man, I don't know what I'd do if I saw them out together. I might just kick his ass. Pound him into the ground with my fists."

"Look, don't go getting into a fight," Lyle looked at his son who took after his mom in the height department. "It won't do you any good to beat some guy up and get yourself into hot water with the law." He saw that Adam liked the fake confidence he was showing in him about being able to win a fist fight. "Maybe you just need to stay away from her. Any girl that does that is a… stank."

"Skank," Mandy corrected her dad from the doorway. "And do you know where you definitely won't run into the skank?" She paused for effect. "College."

CHAPTER 6
Welcome to the Jungle

Adam and Mark were hiking up a wide dirt trail with a large cooler between them. They both held the handles of the twenty-four-can capacity ice chest while walking behind Johnny, Freddy, and his girlfriend Cindy. Sabino Canyon had always been a destination for teens and college kids to come to party on the weekends. They were just a few minutes away from arriving at the *pools*. It was a spot in the canyon where the runoff from the mountains poured down waterfalls into several large pools. The pools were deep enough to swim and offered plenty of space for sunbathing and lounging about. The prickly pear, cholla and saguaro cactus were less prevalent as they moved closer to the pools and streams. They could see up ahead the beginning of palo verde and sycamore trees emerging in patches and groves of welcoming shade.

"Man, it's f'n hot today. I'm sweating like a pig," said Mark as he wiped his brow. He was dressed in a tank top, shorts and high-top sneakers.

"It's not that hot, dude, you're just too fat," said Johnny with his usual insulting honesty.

"Fuck off, Johnny," Mark came back.

"I'm just joking, dude," Johnny laughed his comment off.

"You're just being an ass, Johnny," Cindy told him. She was a year younger than the boys and had been dating Freddy for going on two years. She was attractive, clever, smart and had a knack for keeping Freddy out of trouble. She took on the role of mom for the boys, which she enjoyed as well as being suited for the job.

"I hope we brought enough beer for everyone," Freddy commented.

"It's just the four of us since Johnny isn't drinking," said Adam.

"I brought my doobage." Johnny produced a bag of weed from his shorts. He dangled the clear plastic bag holding the dark green and brown leaves, stems and a few seeds in front of Mark's nose. Mark slapped it away with annoyance.

"Six of us," said Cindy.

"Who else is coming?" asked Adam.

Cindy turned to Freddy. "You didn't tell him?"

"He wouldn't have come if I did."

Adam stopped and looked up to the heavens. Mark abruptly stopped as well as the two of them were stuck with ice chest duty. "Ah shit. Jessica is gonna be there?"

"And Troy," answered Mark.

Adam set down his side of the cooler. He started walking in the other direction.

"Ah, come on man. It's been weeks since you guys broke up," complained Freddy.

"A week. One week! What the hell? I don't want to hang out with them all day. This is going to be so fucking awkward."

"Dude, relax. It's not like they're going to bang in front of you," Johnny said, dishing out more of his patented honesty. Adam stood there looking pissed off, arms crossed over his chest.

Cindy walked up to him and put her hand on his

shoulder. "Look, there are going to be tons of other people at the waterfalls. You know how it is on a Saturday. It's like a giant party. It will be fun. I'm sure we'll barely hang out with them." She batted her large aqua blue eyes at him knowing that Adam had a soft spot for her.

"Besides there will be tons of other pussy there," Johnny said while biting a hangnail on his finger. He looked over at the disgusted look on Cindy's face. "No offense," he told her.

"God, you're a pig."

"Sorry, chicks, there will be tons of other chicks there."

Freddy shook his head at Johnny. "Dude, why don't you have any couth?"

"I said 'no offense' didn't I?"

Adam hesitated then with a sigh said, "Ah, fine." He picked up the other end of the cooler to continue carrying it with Mark. "But they are not drinking any of this beer. Not after I carried it all this way."

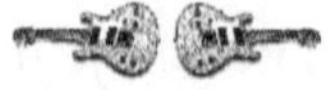

The natural pools formed by the waterfalls were filled with swimmers and sunbathers partying and having a great time. The day was hot, but the water was cool and refreshing. There was not much shade, but the crowd was tanned and used to the Arizona sun kissing their skin with its loving warmth. Music thumped and thrilled from various ghetto blasters that accompanied several large groups as scantily clad young men and woman drank and smoked around the water and dirt beaches.

Tracy and her best friend Loni were lying bikini-clad on towels soaking up the rays and sipping on wine coolers. They were both eye-catching young women, Tracy more classically pretty with a petite frame while Loni could be described as less so but with the body of a bombshell.

Loni tipped her sunglasses down her nose to look at Tracy from heavily made-up eyes. "Please tell me you're going to come back for the summers."

"Of course." Tracy looked over the crowd, then responded with sarcasm, "How could I miss out on this rad scene?"

"Come on, Trace, we've had some great times here. Remember when we stayed way too late, and the sun had set? We were so trashed, and it was so damn dark that we thought we'd never find our way back to the car."

"Oh God, and the coyotes were howling, and it sounded like they were after us. I don't know if I'd classify that as one of the great times, Loni."

"We can laugh about it now. And remember those guys that saved us? They were so cute."

"They were just as lost as we were. We were all just lucky to see car lights in the distance to guide us back," said Tracy dismissively.

"You hate playing the damsel in distress."

"And you love it," said Tracy.

"I can do it so well."

The girls clinked their wine coolers in a toast.

One of the louder boom boxes started blasting *Welcome to the Jungle* by Guns N' Roses. The girls couldn't help but turn to look over at where it was coming from. Standing on a large rock was Troy singing along with the song. Shirtless in white jean shorts, he worked his Axl Rose look to the hilt. He had the same lanky frame as the lead singer to the band and he looked like he was performing for an arena of nonexistent fans.

Welcome to the jungle, we got fun and games
We got everything you want, honey, we know the names
We are the people that can find whatever you may need
If you got the money, honey, we got your disease
It's a jungle, welcome to the jungle
Watch it bring you to your n-n-n-n-n-n-n-n knees, knees
Oh ah, I wanna watch you bleed

Tracy and Loni exchanged a disgusted look.

"This, I'm not going to miss," said Tracy.

On the other side of the pools Jessica lay in a string bikini on a beach towel watching Troy do his Axl Rose thing. Adam, Mark, Freddy, Johnny, and Cindy were standing just yards away watching the performance.

"What the fuck is that?" Mark asked.

"That is what has been doing my girlfriend."

"Ex-girlfriend," Freddy corrected.

"So hot, right, Johnny?" asked Mark.

"Fuck off, dude," Johnny said, punching Mark in the arm.

Cindy slapped Johnny on the back of his head, "Be nice, guys. Come on, let's go have some fun." She led the boys over to Jessica and Troy as the song ended and Troy stepped down off his rock stage. They all greeted each other with s'ups, what ups, and head nods. Adam and Mark set the cooler down and Mark started handing out beers. When he got to Troy he glanced at Adam, not sure if he was serious about not giving Troy any of their beer.

Adam saw this and waved his hand at Mark, "No, no, no. I think I'm owed an apology before we all start sharing beers and pretending like nothing happened. Somebody was wronged here, and it needs to be acknowledged and rectified!"

Jessica stepped in front of Troy toward Adam. "Oh, are you saying you're hurt? You've spent the last few months talking about going away to college but never once said anything about us staying together while you were going to be living up there. You never said that no matter what we can make it work, or that you even wanted it to work! You just whined about leaving your friends behind… and your band."

"You were always part of that equation. I still wanted us to stay together while I was away."

"Really? You never talked about me coming with you next year when *I* graduate," Jessica said with her hands on her hips.

"Come on, Jess, there is no way you could get into NAU with your grades."

"That is so hurtful, Adam. And I don't need to be *in* college to move there," Jessica said with tears welling in her eyes. "You never made me feel like we had a future together."

"I… well, I…" Adam just stammered as he didn't have an answer for her. He just stared at her, and she at him. The others were held captive in the awkward silence.

"So, what's the point? Our breakup was inevitable," Jessica finally said.

Adam hesitated; words still stuck in his mouth. The silence stretched on uncomfortably and the group started to shuffle their feet.

Troy had his head down the whole time and he lifted it up and broke the tension. "I could really use a beer about now… so I sincerely apologize for doing your girlfriend."

Adam looked away from Jessica to Troy. "Whatever, guess she's right, it was inevitable." He turned and walked away, tossing the can of beer over his shoulder that was then caught by Troy. Adam continued walking toward the falls without looking back.

"Well, that was weird. Glad we got past it," Troy said then turned to Jessica. "Uhm, could you see if he brought my Oakleys?"

Tracy and Loni were sitting on their towels, watching the pools and waterfalls. Loni was applying suntan oil on her arms and chest. Her skin glistened in the afternoon sun like dew on a morning flower petal.

"So are Joey and his band playing at the Tucson Gardens next Saturday?"

"Mmhm. The battle of the bands," Tracy said as Loni handed her the suntan enhancing oil. The Tucson Gardens was the hottest live rock club that was anything but a garden. It was an old gray building in the center of a vacant lot incapable of growing a single flower or tree in its dry soil of dirt and rock. The Gardens was the ultimate destination, the one spot in town where every headbanger and up-and-coming band dreamed of rocking out. "Will you come with? I don't think I can handle that freak show by myself."

"I bet they win it this year."

"I don't know… they're barely practicing anymore. Joey has been full time at his mom's car wash. A rock star with a job is hardly a…" Tracy saw someone climbing up the cliffs for a jump spot into the pools. "Looks like we might have a jumper."

Loni turned to see a guy climbing to the top of the eighty-foot-high rock cliff that loomed above the largest pool in the canyon. It was the rare show-off that jumped from the top spot, but the weekends would usually find a few takers that risked life and limb for the rush of that leap. Sometimes during the summer months, the water could be too shallow to allow a safe landing because of the rocky bottom of the pool. She recalled an older guy breaking both his legs two years ago and being airlifted to the hospital.

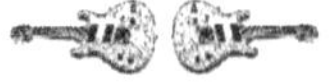

"Your crazy ex is about to kill himself," Troy told Jessica with a head nod to the cliff.

Hearing this they all looked up to see Adam making his way up toward the ledge, stumbling a bit in the process.

"Naw, he always pussies out," Johnny reminded everyone.

Jessica watched Adam make it to the top and stand there at the edge. A worried look crossed her gaze. "Mark, go get him before he does something stupid."

"I'll go with," said Freddy standing up.

Cindy grabbed the back of Freddy's shirt before he could walk away. "Don't you dare jump off that cliff, Fred."

Mark and Freddy began the climb to the top of the cliff with Freddy leading the way. The path was familiar to Freddy as he'd made this jump half a dozen times. Mark had stood at the top a few times to watch someone make the leap but had never done it himself. When they arrived at the top Adam was standing at the edge looking over, down into the dark pool of water wondering how deep it was.

He heard someone coming up behind him and turned to see his friends without surprise.

"Dude, what are you doing?" asked Mark as he came to stand with Adam.

"I've never jumped before. I've been coming here since I was a little kid and I've never jumped. Maybe this is my last shot at it. I go away and maybe I don't ever come back to this place. I always thought I would do it someday. I've stood up here a dozen times and always wussed out."

The sound of people starting to chant, jump, jump, jump came from below. Adam looked out to the crowd and saw all eyes were now on him. He noticed Troy joining in on the chanting while Jessica and Cindy shielded their eyes from the sun as they watched him.

"Yeah, well, half the people that jump end up breaking something on the rocks underneath the water," Mark reminded him.

"Freddy, you've done it. Is it hard?"

Freddy stepped up beside Adam and looked over the

ledge. "You just have to aim for the darkest water. That's the deepest. Then as soon as you hit the water, spread out your arms to slow yourself down before you reach the rocks."

Mark furrowed his brows at Freddy. "Dude, you're not helping."

"I don't want to be afraid to jump. I don't want to be afraid to make a move, a change, take a chance."

"I don't think jumping off a cliff and killing yourself is a good way to start," Mark said.

Adam looked over the water trying to decide if he could see a difference in the water's color to find the deepest part. Mark looked nervously at Freddy to help him talk Adam out of this.

"Why don't you jump from the lower ledge for your first time?" Freddy asked.

"What lower ledge?"

"There's no lower ledge," Mark said.

"Sure. It's about ten feet down. Just climb down the front a bit and you'll see it." Freddy nodded his head toward the ledge. He walked over to Adam and peered further over the edge. He put his hand on Adam's back while standing next to him. They both peered over the side of the rock face to the pool of water below.

"You see that dark spot in the water? That's where you want to go in."

Adam looked to where Freddy was pointing, leaning out a little more to get a good look. Freddy then shoved Adam off the cliff.

"Shhhiiitt!" Adam yelled out as he un-gracefully flailed his arms while falling feet first through the air. His stomach lurched toward his chest as he scrambled, powerless to slow his fall. His sneakered feet hit the water followed by the rest of his body in a giant splash. The cold water sent a shock wave to his senses, and he forgot to break his rate of descent with his arms. Luckily his short stature allowed him to reach the rocks later than someone taller and he was able to find the rocks below and push off them with his feet to ascend to the surface unharmed.

Adam took a huge breath of air and looked up to see Freddy smiling down at him and Mark watching with concern on his face.

"What did you do that for?" Mark asked Freddy.

"He needed that push."

The two boys turned, startled as they heard someone

rushing up behind them. In a blur of tanned skin and long blond hair, a shirtless Johnny went flying past them to leap off the cliff.

"Geronimo!" Johnny cried out as he sailed out over the water to land within a few feet of Adam.

Mark and Freddy leaned back over the cliff to watch Johnny smack into the pool. He went under in a thunder of bubbles and wake, surfacing a few seconds later to whip his hair out of his face. Mark looked down at him with disgust.

Freddy looked over at Mark with the beginnings of a mischievous smile.

"You could use a push too!"

Freddy struggled to push Mark off the ledge but even with the difference in height Mark outweighed him by thirty pounds. Mark easily wrestled Freddy to the edge and pushed him out and over the side. He fell yelling and landed in the water without grace. When he reached back to the surface he attempted to splash Mark from way down below.

Adam, Johnny, and Freddy floated in the water and started taunting Mark to jump in. He looked down at them and shook his head with a satisfied look on his face.

"Come on, fat boy, jump!" called out Johnny.

The crowd hearing this started to chant, fat boy, fat boy. Mark looked on with embarrassment that turned to anger at Johnny as the crowd's calls became louder and louder. He looked down at Johnny's smug smile and grimaced at him. Mark crouched in preparation, then leaped off toward the wading Johnny like he was going to squash him underneath his feet. Johnny and the other boys hastily scattered out of the way. There was a huge splash as Mark hit the water. The crowd loved it, and everyone started cheering as Mark's head broke the water.

The boys pointed and smiled at Mark while praising him and his anger faded. He swam over to Johnny and playfully dunked him and splashed Freddy and Adam.

The music throughout the canyon started back up and everyone resumed their day. The boys made their way out of the water to exit on the far side of the pools. Adam was the last in line behind Mark as they walked past Tracy and Loni who were sitting on their towels watching them.

"Very graceful… fall, Adam," said Tracy.

Adam stopped in surprise, and his face reddened with embarrassment to find Tracy amongst the crowd. He quickly recovered and turned on a bit of faux confidence.

"Well, I'm a trained, professional stuntman."

"As if," Loni quipped.

"Are you?" Tracy said feigning that she was impressed.

Adam and Mark stopped to talk with the girls as Freddy and Johnny walked on with just an encouraging glance back.

Loni lowered her sunglasses to glance up at Mark. "I didn't think you were going to jump, but yours was the best."

"Why, thank you," Mark replied with a smile.

"That really is a scary jump. I didn't know you were some kind of daredevil," said Tracy.

"Sure, just need a push is all," Adam answered her and the four of them smiled at each other. There was a bit of chemistry between Adam and Tracy as well as some galvanic energy linking Mark and Loni.

"Well, all that stunt work has made me mighty thirsty," Mark said pointedly.

"Well, let's get you guys a drink," Loni said, opening their small cooler to grab them fresh bottles.

The boys sat down, sharing the towels with the girls. They wound up hanging out together all day, swimming, talking, laughing, and drinking. Adam found that Tracy habitually socked him in the arm with affection throughout the day enough that he received a flirtatious bruising in that spot. He noticed that Loni had placed her hand on Mark's knee twice and after each time Mark looked over to him like, *is this really happening?* Loni squealed with joy when Mark lifted her up in the water to throw her to splash down like a child in the pool. Adam did his best with Tracy, but it didn't quite have the same effect.

Late in the afternoon Freddy and Cindy walked up to them carrying their gear, looking ready to leave.

"Hey, dicks, you about ready to go? Cindy's got to be at work at six," said Freddy.

"Sorry to break up the party but you guys drove," Cindy said holding onto Freddy's arm.

"Okay, take a chill pill," Adam said, then turned to Tracy. "Are you guys going to the Taylor brothers' party tomorrow night?"

"Mhmhm, hopefully we'll see you there."

Mark turned to Loni, a bit unsure how to end the day. "Thanks for the coolers. Next time the drinks are on us."

"I'm counting on it," she answered coyly.

The boys walked away with Cindy and Freddy toward their group. Cindy hip-bumped Adam along the way.

"I told you that you'd have fun today," she told him.

Adam spotted Troy, Jessica and Johnny waiting for them. Jessica was glaring at him while holding on to Troy's hand. A slight, satisfied smile crossed Adam's lips. "Couldn't have worked out better," he said to himself.

CHAPTER 7

Sorority Sister

Loni's Pontiac Firebird idled noisily outside Tracy's house as the girls said their goodbyes. Tracy grabbed her bag and towel and exited the car in her cut-off shorts and bikini top. She eyed Ron, her mom's boyfriend, in the driveway washing her mom's late model BMW. She heard Loni's car drive off in a roar of souped-up exhaust as she approached Ron in his wet tank top, bare feet, and shorts. He was thirty something with receding blond hair and long sideburns, tan and attractive. She didn't care for him during the first few months of their romance as the guy was like ten years younger than her mom. But he had grown on her as he was pretty cool and not a total creeper like she originally thought.

"How was the canyon?"

"It was actually pretty rad today."

"Oh yeah? Sweet. Well, your mom is a little on the high-strung side today. Just so you know."

Tracy stopped and looked apprehensively at the front door.

"Thanks for the heads-up." She took a deep breath and started up the walkway.

"Something about a sorority."

"Great," Tracy replied with a hand wave.

Tracy came through the front door and made a bee line toward her bedroom. Her mom, Barbara, was in the kitchen chopping vegetables for something she was making for dinner. She spotted Tracy trying to escape to her room without a greeting.

"Sweetie, I'm so glad you're home. I've got the best news!" Barbara saw by the look on her daughter's face that she was completely uninterested, but she decided to push through it in hopes of engaging her. "What is the top sorority at ASU? Pi Beta Phi of course. Well, it just so happens that a friend of mine at the country club, Pamela, has a daughter that will be a senior this year at ASU and is, surprise—the membership chair! And guess what?"

Barbara knew better than to wait for an answer with Tracy. "She is going to have her daughter recommend you as a pledge! Isn't that great? You're going to be a shoo-in for the sisterhood!"

Tracy stopped in her tracks and spun toward her mother. "Mom, gag me. I told you I don't want to be in a sorority. Why would I want to spend four years in a house with a bunch of snobby bitches?"

"Tracy! I'm trying to help you." Barbara's voice rose two octaves higher with emotion. "You don't understand what a leg up this would be for you. You would build friendships with a higher caliber of girls then you have now, not just friends, sisters. You would also meet boys. Boys who come from good families! Boys who will become doctors, lawyers, congressmen. Tracy, sweetie, this is for your own good."

"This has nothing to do with me! You're talking

about *your* dreams, what *you* want. Yes, I want to go to college. Yes, I want to get a good education, but I want to meet *real* people. I'll make my own friends, Mom. Stop crawling up my butt about this."

"Oh, sure, like the sluts and burnouts you hang around with now, right?"

"At least they're not pretending to be something they're not!"

Tracy stomped down the hallway and into her bedroom. Barbara flinched as the slamming door loudly reverberated throughout the house.

"Well, you can just stay in there for the rest of the summer!" She started aggressively chopping the vegetables. She then yelled out to be heard in the driveway, "Ron! Ron! Come fix me a Long Island iced tea! My daughter is driving me to drink."

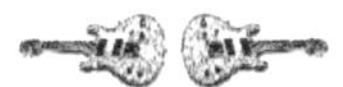

Adam lay on a plastic blow-up raft floating in the middle of his pool. It was a hot, late Sunday morning and he was happily soaking up some rays. He cracked one eye open under his sunglasses to check on Mark, who was sitting on a lounge chair talking on a cordless phone.

His sister, Mandy, walked over to the other side of the pool with a ghetto blaster. She popped in a David Bowie cassette. She pressed play and walked over to the edge of the pool as *Let's Dance* began to play. She lip-synced the song and mimicked the dance that Bowie did while performing the song on MTV.

Let's dance, put on your red shoes and dance the blues
Let's dance, to the song they're playing on the radio
Let's sway, while color lights up your face
Let's sway, sway through the crowd to an empty space

Adam watched her for a few moments then paddled closer to where she was dancing at the edge of the pool and started to splash her. She jumped in, making a cannon ball but failed to splash him back. She dove under the water then swam up underneath and tipped him off the raft. They began play-fighting, and he dunked her; both laughed and were having fun.

Mark hung up the phone and pushed the antenna down. Adam threw Mandy up and away from him and swam over to the shallow end to talk with him.

"So, how did it go?"

"Well, we talked for a while…"

"We noticed," Mandy cut in.

"And then I brought up the Taylor brothers' party…"

"And what did she say?" Adam asked impatiently.

"Yeah, and am I invited to this?" Mandy asked with anticipation.

"As if!" answered Adam with an annoyed look at his sister. He splashed her and she splashed back.

"Can I just finish my story?" asked Mark. "She wanted to know if I would pick her up and take her to the party."

"Yes! Dude, you're in like Flynn."

"Did she say it was a date?" Mandy asked, piping in. The boys looked at her like, *of course, it's a date*. "Maybe she just needs a ride. Maybe her other ride bailed. You should have confirmed it was a date. I heard she was seeing some guy named Craig."

"Don't listen to her, dude. She is messing with your head. It's totally a date."

Mark stepped away, to think about his conversation with Loni. "Shit. What if she's right? Damn, I can't call her back and ask. I'd seem like a dweeb."

"Total dweeb," Mandy agreed.

Mark turned to Adam. "Dude, you have to come with me." Adam shook his head.

"Seems kind of awkward, man."

"No, you've got to come now. If it's not a date it will make it totally casual."

"And if it's a date?" Adam asked.

"I'll be like—yeah, I don't know why he came. He's in a bad spot, getting cheated on and all."

Mandy nodded her head in agreement with Mark. "Yeah, like he's totally pathetic. The truth is always the best route."

Adam turned to his sister and made a face. She stuck her tongue out at him, and he pounced on her, dunking her under the water. Mark ran to the edge of the pool and cannonballed both of them.

Tracy was rummaging through her closet looking for something to wear. She held up two different tops to her chest to see how they looked in the mirror. She frowned and tossed them both into the growing pile on the floor. She picked up a thigh-length dress and held that against her.

"That is a good shade of blue on you," her mom said from the doorway, watching her. Tracy looked at her mom and tossed it on the floor. She then picked up a pair of white jeans from the pile of discards and started to put them on.

"Ron and I are going out to dinner at the club with the Walkers, I don't suppose you'd like to come? Their son Craig is going to be there."

"Sorry, Mom, I'm going out with Joey to a party."

"You know, the last time we saw Craig he was asking about you. He has grown into a total babe. It wouldn't kill you to branch out a little. See someone new," Barbara told her with enthusiasm.

Tracy looked up from her dressing with disgust. "Mom, Craig Walker is a sleazebag. He drives a Corvette and has slept with half the girls at your precious club… including some of the moms.

"Well, who could blame them? He's quite a catch," Barbara said unperturbed.

"Well, he sounds more like your type. Why don't you give Ron the night off and get yourself a new boy toy?"

Barbara's face darkened. "Don't be so rude, Tracy. I'm just trying to help you as always. If you don't start taking some of my advice, you'll wind up knocked up by some hippie who washes cars for a living." Barbara left the doorway and walked loudly down the hall.

"Joey doesn't wash the cars! His family owns the car wash!" Tracy yelled at her retreating mother. "And no one says hippie anymore!"

CHAPTER 8
Lost Boys

It was a sunny afternoon as Mark and Adam were finishing up washing Mark's mustard yellow VW bug outside of Adam's house when Freddy and Johnny drove up in Freddy's car and rolled down the windows. Adam looked up and tossed the towel down he was using to dry the fender of the car.

"Hey, studs," Johnny called to them.

"What are you guys up to?" Adam asked as he approached the window.

"Hop in. We're going trestling," answered Johnny with a wide grin and slapped Freddy's shoulder to tell the details.

"Yeah, Robert told us about a spot that is just like the scene in *Lost Boys.* Come on, we're going to go check it out."

"No shit? That's way cool."

Adam and Mark hopped in the back of the car and Freddy revved the engine and cranked up his stereo. He slapped the gear shift into drive and peeled out on his way down the street.

The car turned off onto a dirt road twenty minutes later and Freddy's car took a beating as he navigated his way down the rutted desert road that was meant for off-roading vehicles rather than Freddy's muscle car. A cloud of dirt followed behind them as they approached train tracks in the distance that spanned a canyon attached to a fifty-yard trestle-like bridge.

Freddy spun the car into a power slide stop as he got within walking distance of the tracks. A cloud of dust wafted through the car's open windows and the boys issued complaints about Freddy's bone-headed parking job. They exited the car with a bit of coughing and spitting of dust.

"Smooth move, Ex-Lax," Johnny told him as he brushed dirt out of his hair.

The train tracks lay in the middle of the desertscape stretching for miles in either direction. The terrain was like a sparse forest of saguaro cacti and palo verde trees. Low rises broke up the landscape of the desert floor.

The boys started walking toward the train tracks then followed them to the edge of the deep ravine that lay underneath the bridge stretching across. The trestle was constructed of sturdy, rusted steel and the drop from the center was about forty feet. Johnny started to lead them down the tracks and over the ravine. Mark stopped at the edge of the trestle. Adam turned and looked back at his friend.

"What's wrong?"

Mark looked over the side then back down the length of the tracks. "This is stupid. We shouldn't be here."

"Come on, fat boy. Don't be such a chicken," Johnny said, looking over his shoulder.

"Dude, it's just like the *Lost Boys*. All you have to do

is climb down and hold on while the train goes over," Freddy said, turning to look at the worried look on Mark's face.

"That was a movie, you idiot. Those guys didn't really do that. It was totally fake. I'm not going to fall and kill myself to reenact a stupid movie."

Adam furrowed his brows at Mark. "Stupid movie? That movie was amazing."

"No doubt," agreed Johnny. "Really dude, you can be such a…"

Suddenly they noticed movement in the distance behind Mark. The track started to vibrate under their sneakers. A train was coming fast from around a bend in the track. Mark looked behind as he saw the shock on their faces. He hurried back to the edge of the trestle and down off the tracks a safe distance away.

"Shit! Let's go," Freddy said as he started to climb over the side of the tracks and onto the structure of the trestle. The other boys rushed over to where he was descending and waited for their turn to go over the side.

"Shit! Shit!" Adam said, wanting to hurry Johnny along so he could get off the track and still stay near the other two boys. The thick metal beams crisscrossed throughout the structure and offered plenty of handholds to traverse down and across. The boys moved further down the beams. Adam glanced off to see Mark climbing a large flat rock to get a better view of them from his vantage point.

"You guys are going to get yourselves killed!" Mark yelled at them as he stood watching, head on a swivel as the train barreled down the tracks closer and closer.

Finally, Freddy, Johnny, and Adam reached the lower support girders and hung from them, feet dangling in the air. The train could be heard now, getting louder and louder to their ears. The trestle began to vibrate noisily as it drew nearer.

"Oh my God, oh my God!" Adam exclaimed as he looked down below him, then back up at the excited, as well as terrified faces of Freddy and Johnny.

The train had almost reached the ravine and the vibration started to affect Adam's grip. He tried to swing his legs back up to cling to the beam for support.

"Dude, you can't go back up!" Freddy yelled at him over the noise of the train.

The conductor noticed the parked car and a heavyset boy standing on a rock watching and blew the train's whistle loudly.

"Hang on!" Johnny hollered out.

Adam dropped his legs back down and gripped the metal for dear life. The train drove over the tracks above them, and the violent shaking and vibration threatened to knock them all off their perch.

The boys were yelling and screaming in fear and exhilaration. Broad smiles and wide eyes met each other's looks. The train engine and its thirty or so cars finally passed by, and the boys continued to hang on as the vibration faded away with the now distant engine noise.

They all began to laugh in relief, relishing their bravery.

Mark hopped off his rock and started to walk over to them shaking his head. "Idiots." He made his way to the slope off the tracks leading down into the narrow canyon so that he could see the three boys hanging off the girders.

Johnny swung his body toward Adam and locked his legs around his. Adam squirmed to unhitch Johnny's legs and tightened his grip on the metal.

"Quit messing, dude!" Adam protested.

Freddy spotted Mark looking at them from the top of the slope. "Mark, you pussy. You missed it. That was some crazy shit."

"Yeah, crazy shit. Why don't you jump down now, *Lost Boys?*" Mark rolled his eyes as he now saw that they were hanging from the trestle a mere four or five feet from the sloping ground of the side of the ravine. The boys let go and easily dropped down to the dirt incline unharmed. The three of them started climbing up toward Mark.

"Oh man, that was amazing," said Adam out of breath.

"Yeah, amazing," Mark said with a heavy dose of sarcasm.

"I didn't see you hanging off the tracks, fat boy," Johnny snarked.

"You guys were barely off the ground."

"That is a very steep slope! We could have slid all the way to the bottom if we fell," Freddy said, pushing by Mark.

"Yeah, terrifying. Can we head back now?" Mark answered and followed the others back to the waiting car.

"What? You got a hot date or something?" Johnny asked.

"As a matter of fact, I do, dickhead."

"Your cousin back in town?"

"Fuck off. I'm taking Loni to the party tonight."

Johnny looked over at Adam to see if that was true. Adam nodded his head.

"Whoa! Hell yes, fat boy, we got to get home and scrub you down." Johnny ran over to Mark and grabbed him around the waist from behind and with effort lifted him and attempted to run with him toward the car.

"Put me down, you idiot!" Mark said as the other boys joined in with Johnny to carry Mark to the car.

"Let's get this virgin ready to get laid!" Johnny yelled and they all struggled to not drop Mark.

CHAPTER 9

Where's Tubbs?

Mark and Adam drove up to Loni's house in his freshly washed and vacuumed bug. They were both dressed up in their coolest *Miami Vice*-inspired outfits of T-shirts underneath pastel colored sport jackets. Adam hung back a bit as Mark approached the front door and rang the bell.

They waited almost a minute and Mark was about to knock on the wooden door when it opened in front of him. Donny, Loni's older brother, stood in front of

Mark with a confused furrow to his brow. He towered over Mark sporting a military-style crew cut and a square jaw. Donny's olive gray T-shirt was stretched tight over his muscular chest.

"Hey, I'm Mark, is Loni home?" His voice cracked to a squeak on the last word.

"She's here, are you the dude driving her to this party?"

"Um, yeah. Is she ready?"

Donny looked closely at Mark. "How old are you?"

"Eighteen."

"Clean driving record?"

"Um, yeah."

Donny relaxed a bit. "Good. She's not ready yet. How about a beer while you wait?"

Mark blew out a bit of breath in relief. He was a little unsure of himself but said, "Ahh, sure."

Donny's demeanor quickly switched to aggression. "Ahh, sure? The answer is *no*! No, you do not want a beer. You are not twenty-one. You are responsible for driving my little sister tonight. You will not touch a beer, not a single. Fucking. Drop. Of. Alcohol." Mark took a step back as Donny came further out of the doorway. "You and your little stoner friend over there are to take good care of my sister and keep her safe tonight. If she comes back harmed, drunk, scared, or unhappy I'm going to crush the both of you into a spewing pile of shit pus."

Mark started to back away as Donny closed in holding out his hand with his palm up. "Hand me your license."

Mark quickly pulled his wallet out of his pants pocket and took out his driver's license. Donny snapped it up and looked it over for five seconds, closed his eyes momentarily, then looked down at Mark, handing it back.

"I've memorized everything, your address on Bellevue Street, date of birth, social security number, everything. Just like that, because I keep my mind and body clean. And speaking of clean, you will have clean, pure thoughts in the company of my sister. You even *think* about violating her and I will rip your head off and mount it above our fireplace. Loni is an innocent, naïve girl and I expect her to be returned as such." He looked hard at Mark. "You got it?" He quickly turned toward Adam. "You got me too, Ozzy?"

Adam nodded his head yes. Just then, out came Loni

dressed in the smallest skirt that seemed possible, along with high heels and a cropped top revealing an inch or two of her midriff. She had on a heavy makeup and her hair was teased up big and bitchin' like she had just stepped out of a fashion magazine.

She breezed by Donny, grabbing Mark's hand on her way. "Hi, Mark. Bye, Donny, see you later."

She passed by a staring Adam who glanced uncomfortably at Donny.

"Hi, Adam."

"Hi, Loni," Adam croaked.

Loni leaned over to whisper in Mark's ear, "Why's he riding with us?"

Mark whispered back, "Got cheated on, totally damaged. Wouldn't take a hint. We'll lose him at the party."

CHAPTER 10
For Those About to Rock

Mark slowed down the car as he drove up to the raging house party. Cars lined the street for blocks. There were late teens and young twenties milling about the neighborhood. Music could be heard through the open car windows as he got closer. He passed the Taylor brothers' large, two-story house and saw a spot just big enough to squeeze his VW bug into. Mark jumped out, leaving his door open for Adam to get out of the back seat and hurried to open Loni's door.

"Thank you, Marky, you're so sweet," Loni said as she slipped herself out of the little car; while watching her skirt to make sure not too much was revealed. Mark's eyes had major trouble looking away from those long legs as she exited.

Loni held out her hand for Mark to take and they started up the sidewalk toward the party house. Adam third-wheeled it just behind Mark.

"So, Loni, is Tracy coming by herself?" Adam asked with a hopeful tone.

"I think she is coming with Joey."

"That's cool," Adam replied with a hint of despondency.

Loni saw someone she knew standing near the front of the house and went off to greet them.

Mark put his arm around Adam's shoulder and quietly said, "Don't blow this for me by killing the mood."

"I won't."

"Look, I don't know why she likes me, but it seems like she does. This kind of thing doesn't ever happen for me like it happens for you."

Adam looked at Mark and saw the vulnerability in Mark that he hadn't ever noticed before. "Dude, you've been my best friend since second grade. I know fifty million reasons why she likes you."

Mark chuckled after a second and sarcastically joked to him, "Don't make this all about you."

They caught up to Loni and the three of them entered the front door.

Oingo Boingo blasted throughout the house from an expensive hi-fi stereo and Bose speakers. The downstairs living room was full of partygoers mingling, dancing, moving from one room to another. A group of boys that Adam recognized as the varsity football team from last year were gathered around the sofas engaged in an arm-wrestling match on the coffee table. Red plastic cups and bottles of beer coated every surface throughout the house. A keg of beer that could be seen in the kitchen had a line of teens waiting for their turn.

Tim Taylor, the taller of the two fraternal twins hosting the party, spotted Adam and Mark on his way from the bathroom. He looked like he stepped out of *Surfer* magazine in his Hang Ten T-shirt, board shorts, and Vans. Tim's sun-bleached hair and tanned skin looked like he spent his days riding waves even though he lived over three hundred miles from the nearest beach.

"Looks like a bitchin' party, Tim," Mark told him.

"I know, right? Thomas is getting a little freaked out that it's gotten so big."

"Your brother worries too much," said Adam.

Just then a guy with long hair and an Iron Maiden shirt slid down the banister colliding with a guy in an old football jersey. A shoving match ensued but it was quickly over as several bystanders broke it up before it could escalate.

"Maybe your brother shouldn't have invited the whole football team," noted Mark.

"Well, he's still bros with all of them."

"Headbangers and jocks on roids may not be the best mix," Adam said.

Loni, who was becoming bored with the conversation put her hands around Mark's arm. "I'm thirsty, Marky."

Mark smiled widely at her then led her toward the kitchen and said over his shoulder, "We'll catch you later."

Adam and Tim looked at each other and Tim mouthed 'Marky?'. Adam just rolled his eyes and shook his head.

Thomas, the shorter, stockier version of his twin brother Tim walked up to them in a panic.

"I heard there was a fight. What happened? Did anything break?"

"No biggie, nothing happened, mellow out," Tim said.

"I'm going to lock all the doors upstairs. Make sure no one is stealing anything." Thomas hurried up the stairs as Adam and Tim stared after him.

"So paranoid," Adam remarked.

"Let's go out back. Freddy and all of them are there and we have a whole cooler of choice beer."

The boys threaded their way through the crowd and out the sliding glass door to the backyard. There was a large kidney-shaped pool with wide decking scattered with lounge chairs and patio tables. This was where the smokers, punks, and headbangers hung out in several groups. Rock music blared from a ghetto blaster on the counter of a built-in BBQ. Adam and Tim spotted Freddy with Cindy, Johnny, a girl named Melissa and a guy named Derek who had his foot on top of a large ice chest.

Johnny was smoking a cigarette in his unique way, holding it like a joint, but with his palm over the top rather than underneath. He spotted Adam walking over and looked him up and down.

"Hey, Crockett, where's Tubbs?"

"Ha. Ha. Hey, Melissa." Adam brushed by Johnny to embrace Melissa in a friendly hug.

"He's inside with his date. Loni," said Tim, answering Johnny's question.

Derek let out a whistle. "Way to go, Mark. Loni's hotter than a jalapeño pepper."

"Got a beer for me in that cooler, Derek?" Adam asked.

Derek grabbed a beer bottle from the cooler and handed it over. "You betcha."

Adam turned the green toned beer bottle in his hand. "Oooh, a Heineken."

"That's right, nothing but the best."

Derek and Adam clinked their bottles together. Melissa looked over at Adam and made a concerned face at him.

"So how are you hanging in there, Adam?"

Cindy piped in before Adam could answer, "Oh, he's doing fine. He's trying to hook up with Tracy Smith."

"We are just friends," he corrected her.

"So, you're totally over Jessica now?" Melissa asked.

"Totally."

"Good, cause she's over there."

Melissa pointed out Jessica, dressed ridiculously hot sitting around a patio table with Troy and a few other teens. Troy was dressed in full rock star mode, bandanas on his jeans that were ripped in all the cool places, sleeveless jean jacket, and cowboy boots. He looked more like Jon Bon-Jovi tonight then Axl Rose. Adam cringed in secret jealousy that this guy could morph into the coolest band leaders.

"Oh my God, is that guy the biggest poser on the planet or what?" Adam said.

Melissa looked over at Troy and ran her tongue over her red painted lips. "Maybe, but he sure is hot."

"He's not even…" Adam started to say.

"In a band," both Cindy and Melissa finished Adam's sentence at the same time.

"Yes, we know already. You guys are actual rock

stars," continued Cindy, addressing Adam, Johnny, and Freddy.

"We just need a gig," Johnny said dismissively.

"We'd kill," Freddy agreed.

The band members high fived each other.

"Well, you guys are playing at the battle of the bands, right? The one at the Tucson Gardens?" asked Derek.

"We should totally enter," Freddy said excitedly.

Adam looked a little nervously at Johnny and could see some apprehension in his eyes as well. "I don't know if we're ready for that," Adam said.

"Definitely not," Cindy agreed.

Derek's face showed growing confusion. "But, I thought you guys already entered? Your band is on the flyer."

"What flyer?"

"It was on my car when I went out to get a lighter." Derek pulled a folded flyer from his back pocket and handed it to Adam. "Somebody must have put them out earlier. I saw them on everyone's cars."

Adam opened the piece of paper and Johnny, Tim, and Freddy leaned in to see it. It had a list of ten band names with the Bellevue Boys at the bottom. The date, time and location were listed, and it looked professionally printed.

"Bellevue Boys, that's you guys, right?" asked Tim.

"Yeah," said Johnny quietly.

"Who entered us?" Adam asked.

The boys looked at each other questioningly. Each had a baffled look on their face.

"Maybe Mark did," offered Melissa.

"You think?" Adam questioned Johnny.

"Let's go find lover boy and ask him."

The boys took off toward the house and had to pass by Troy and Jessica. Jessica was smirking at Adam as they hurried by. They headed through the family room looking for Mark, and Freddy spotted him at the kitchen table playing quarters with Loni, Tracy, and Joey. Before they could start questioning Mark there were several greetings between the two groups. Tracy smiled at Adam and said hi, and he smiled uncomfortably back as Joey stared him down.

"Oh look, Sonny Crockett showed up," he said, goofing on Adam's outfit.

Tracy gave him an elbow into his side and quietly said, "Joey, be nice."

Adam leaned down next to Mark and from the side of his mouth asked, "Dude, did you enter us in the battle of the bands?"

"What? Why would I do that?"

Adam slapped the flyer down on the table in front of Mark. "These are all over everyone's cars out front."

"What the fuck?" Mark said as he saw their band name at the bottom.

Loni looked over and saw the flyer. "Marky! Are you going to play? That is so cool."

Tracy leaned forward to look as well. "That's awesome, guys! Joey and his band are playing as well. It'll be so much fun."

Joey edged up to see the names on the sheet. "Bellevue Boys? Are you guys even any good?"

Johnny, Freddy, Mark, and Adam looked at each other. No one wanted to answer that question.

Loni, grabbed Mark's hand. "Well, I'll be your first groupie."

The table settled into an awkward silence and Joey leaned back and rolled his eyes. "Whatever. Are we gonna play some quarters or what?"

Adam moved from car to car collecting the flyers off their windshields for the battle of the bands. He was so focused on taking them all down that he didn't notice that the beat-up car whose hood he was reaching over had a familiar old surfboard on top strapped to its luggage rack. He was in the act of removing the flyer when a hand grabbed his from the rolled-down window.

"Hey, thief!" Ricky said loudly, startling his friend and workmate.

"Fuck!" Adam cried out and jumped back.

Ricky hung his head out the window, smiling a stoner's high smile.

"Dude, you freaked me out. Don't do that again, you're going to give me a heart attack. Either that or I'm going to bust ass just off instinct."

"Hop in, little buddy," Ricky said.

Adam climbed into the passenger seat and dropped the stack of flyers on the floor to lie cluttered with empty fast food wrapping and soda cans. The car's interior smelled of a mixture of pot smoke, French fries, and mildew.

Ricky pointed at the flyers. "Doing community service?"

Adam picked up one and handed it to Ricky. "Trying to head off some major embarrassment. Someone entered my band into this."

"Cool. You guys could win five hundred dollars," said Ricky as he read over the details.

"I don't know if we are ready to play for an audience."

"Everyone will be so drunk or high, it will be fine. Don't worry, be happy," Ricky reasoned and handed Adam the pipe and lighter for a toke.

Adam sighed heavily and lighted the bowl of marijuana, taking a long slow hit. He leaned his head on the back of the seat and stared at the battle of the bands flyer.

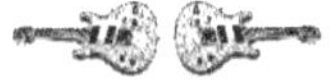

Tracy, Joey, Mark, and Loni were engaged in a sloppy game of quarters. The kitchen table had puddles of spilt and sloshed beer, and they each had a cup in front of them. Tracy rolled a quarter off her nose that bounced perfectly into a cup then signaled Joey to drink. Loni then bounced the quarter into her cup with a high-pitched squeal after it plopped right in. She pointed her long-painted fingernail at Mark.

"No, not me. I have to drive you home. I think I'm done."

"Ah, come on, Tubbs," Joey said, "don't be such a wuss."

"He's not being a wuss. He's being a gentleman," Tracy retorted.

"Yeah Joey, you drink it," Loni said pointing her finger at Joey.

Joey picked up the cup and downed the beer. He then, with a drunken grin, spit out the quarter to bounce in front of Mark.

"Gross, Joey," the girls said in unison.

Joey turned to Mark and squinted his eyes at him. "So, do you guys wear yamakas on stage?"

"As if," said Loni defensively.

"You're being an ass," Tracy said, a hint of real anger showing in her voice.

"What? Him and your new puppy dog Adam are Jew boys. Jews that rock," he finished with a heavy note of sarcasm.

"Jews can rock. Hello… Kiss," Mark said.

"Kiss sucks."

Mark counted the fingers on his hand. "Come on, Rush, David Lee Roth…"

"The Ramones," Tracy added.

"Bob Dylan," listed Loni.

"Dylan is not a Jew," said Joey with an eye roll.

"He's a big-time Jew, Joey," Tracy affirmed.

"Huge," said Mark.

Joey pushed himself away from the table drunkenly. "What the fuck? You guys all suck. I'm so sick of this shit. Your stupid band is gonna get creamed at the Gardens. We'll see who can rock." He got up from the table and stumbled away. He spotted two hotly dressed girls and approached them. Tracy watched as he gave them hugs and conversed a few moments, then left with his arm around one of the girls who seemed to be into him.

"What's his problem," Loni asked.

"He's just unhappy," Tracy answered as Joey exited out of her view.

"He's right though, we're not very good. I don't even know how we got on that lineup."

"Well, Tracy and I will cheer you on. Right, Tracy?"

"Yeah. It may kill my relationship but it's kind of on life support as it is."

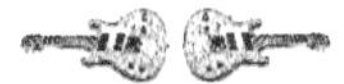

Adam and Ricky were still sitting in Ricky's car passing the pipe back and forth between them. Adam's stress level had reverted to its customary state of 'I'm not entirely sure what I'm doing with my life, but for now, fuck it.'

"So, you guys didn't even have to audition for this?"

"I don't even know how we got picked. Maybe we could ask someone who works at the Gardens, but that would be a weird conversation. We could just not show up."

"Dude, maybe someone or something is looking out for you. There could be a higher purpose for you to perform that night." Ricky started leaning into his philosophical mojo. "This was meant to be. You must follow all of life's paths. The universe has put you on this course. You're obligated to follow it through. Don't fuck with the universe, grasshopper."

"Dude, that was very profound," Adam said, taking another hit on the pipe.

"These ideas flow through me like the tides of the ocean."

The two boys looked toward the front door of the Taylor house as Joey exited with a couple of guys and girls, with one wrapped in his arm. They walked by Ricky's car and Joey noticed Adam in the front seat. Joey stopped and glared at him and gave him the finger before continuing on his way. They hopped into a souped-up Mustang, peeling out and driving away.

"I think Joey profoundly hates me."

"That guy hates the world. No need to feel singled out." Ricky took a long drag off the pipe and held the smoke in for several seconds. He slowly blew out a cloud of smoke rings. "You've been dressing like a rock star since you started high school, now it's time to act like one."

"You've been dressing like a surfer since high school and driving with an old board on your car for years, but you've never even left Arizona."

"I'm a surfer of the mind, little buddy," Ricky quipped, conjuring a small smoke ring he had somehow tucked away before lifting his brows at Adam, a mischievous glint in his eyes.

The Taylor brothers' party was reaching the tipping point of becoming a full-on rager. The music was getting harder, the crowd was getting louder, and

Thomas was moving through the living room, head on a swivel, nerves teetering on edge. He looked up the stairway to see two girls coming down with boas and fox fur stoles wrapped around themselves, lit cigarettes dangled from their lips.

"Those are my mom's! What the hell are you doing in my parents' room!" Thomas grabbed the items off the girls and wrapped them in a protective ball in his arms. He then spotted two boys standing outside his father's office smoking cigars and holding their cups of alcohol while chatting. He stomped over to them.

"Where did you get these cigars? Are these my dad's?" Thomas turned to address the entire crowd, yelling to be heard over the music, "I thought I said the office was off limits!"

His brother Tim, Johnny and Freddy walked up to him with concerned looks.

"What's going on, Thomas?" asked Tim.

"This fucking party is getting out of control. We gotta get everyone out of here. Now!"

Johnny looked around at the crowd. "You can't kick all these people out."

"You'll seem like a total dick," Freddy agreed.

"These people are going to destroy our house," Thomas said, almost pleading with his brother.

"You could call the police on yourself, no one would probably know it was you," suggested Johnny.

"It's not that bad," said Tim dismissively.

Just then a girl ran through the living room spraying champagne on two guys as they laughed and ran away from her. They continued their unruly exit, leaving a trail of splashing chaos in their wake as they dashed toward the front door.

A couple of football players grabbed an autographed football that was sitting near a set of trophies off the fireplace mantel and started passing it around. Thomas began to lose his shit.

"That's it, God damn it!" Thomas yelled out as he then started climbing the stairs muttering angrily to himself.

Tim grabbed the arm of one of the football players and said, "All right, could you guys take it outside?"

The players took that as a great idea and piled out the front door bringing a large crowd of people with them. Tim, Johnny, and Freddy followed, ushering more partygoers in hopes of clearing the house further.

The front of the house was now fast becoming the place to be. Adam exited Ricky's car and found his friends outside with a group. Mark, Loni and Tracy emerged from within the crowd and found Adam. 'For Those About to Rock' by AC/DC was blaring from one of the nearby car stereos. Just before the song was about to ring out with cannon fire effects, Thomas arrived in the front doorway, a crazed look in his eyes, toting a pump-action shotgun. He took a couple of steps into the yard as several people noticed him and cringed away.

Thomas racked a shell into the chamber and fired the rifle into the air in unison with the song's cannon fire.

BLAM!

The crowd paused all movement in shock at what had just happened.

Thomas stood, glaring from one group of teens to another, then pumped another round with the slide.

The crowd exploded into panic with everyone running or diving for cover.

Thomas screamed out, "Get out of here!" and fired another round perfectly timed to the next cannon fire of the AC/DC song. There was a frantic scramble by everyone as they rushed to their cars, and police sirens began to wail in the distance.

Time slowed for Tracy as she stood in shock, watching as Thomas racked the shotgun again. Adam grabbed her arm and pulled her toward Mark's bug along with Loni and Mark. The four of them piled quickly into the car. The VW's engine roared to life and lurched out of its spot between two cars that were in the midst of starting their own engines. Mark gunned the accelerator down the block. He took the first turn, fishtailing the squat back end. And within the next thirty seconds he put them safely blocks away from the mayhem.

Tracy and Adam watched through the back window as they left the neighborhood, finally breathing a sigh of relief before facing forward. Adam watched Mark's wide eyes as he kept checking the rear-view mirror for trouble.

"Holy shit. Thomas is insane," said Adam.

"What the hell was that all about?" asked Tracy as her nerves settled.

"Thomas was getting paranoid and wanted everyone to leave."

"He could have just asked," remarked Loni with a

head shake.

Adam turned to Tracy as a thought occurred to him. "Shit, Joey's not going to be able to find you."

"Then, he shouldn't have gone on a beer run with those skanks. He'd drunk too much already if you ask me," answered Loni.

"Yeah. He was starting to be a dick," Mark added.

"Starting?" Adam quipped sarcastically. He looked to see Tracy staring out the window at nothing. "Sorry, Tracy. That wasn't cool."

After a moment Tracy shook off the dark thoughts running through her head. "Well, now what? Call it a night?"

"It's still early," complained Loni.

"Well, what then?" asked Mark of the small group.

They drove in silence for a moment, then Adam's face lit up with an idea. "Donuts?"

Mark looked at Adam in the rear-view mirror and Spocked an eyebrow. "Donuts?"

"Donuts?" Tracy asked.

"I'm not hungry," Loni said.

"He doesn't mean those kinds of donuts," Mark said with a smile.

The girls were confused, and Adam broke out in a wide grin, starting a chant, "Donuts, donuts, donuts."

Loni was unsure what was going on but was up for any sort of fun. She joined in the chant with Adam, "Donuts, donuts, donuts."

"All right, all right," said Mark and he made a sharp turn down a different street heading toward the edge of town.

Tracy leaned over to Adam, "What's the deal with donuts?"

"You'll see."

CHAPTER 11

Donuts

Mark settled into the worn driver's seat of the idling VW, the hum of the engine barely audible over the vast silence of the desert night. Despite the lateness of the hour, he slid on his mirrored aviator sunglasses. The headlights cast a narrow beam across the expansive, grassless field they had ventured onto from a seemingly endless dirt road that disappeared into the darkness behind them.

He turned to Loni wearing a serious expression. "Roll up the windows, things are about to get 'off the wall.'"

Loni hastily rolled her window up and Mark started gunning the engine.

Adam started chanting 'donuts' again with Loni and Tracy quickly joining in.

Mark held the clutch in and smoothly moved the stick shift into gear. He pressed his foot on the accelerator, engine roaring. "Hang on!" He popped the clutch and the VW rocketed forward. Mark cranked the wheel and floored it, and the car began to spin. They were all shoved against one side of the little car as the engine screamed out while the car twisted in a tight circle doing donuts.

The stereo was blasting music, and the car was creating a huge dust cloud that enveloped them completely until they were blinded by the blurring headlights in the brown haze of dirt and dust. Mark spun the car for almost a minute then let it coast to a stop, immersed in the dissipating brown cloud. He looked over at his passengers who were all wide-eyed and full of smiles and laughter.

"That was awesome! Do it again," said Loni giving

Mark a playful shove.

"Hang on, I think Tracy needs a turn," Adam said.

"What? No, I don't know how."

Adam motioned for everyone to get out and switch seats. Tracy was protesting but with a huge smile on her face. Mark let Tracy into the driver's seat and he and Loni hopped in the back. Adam slid into the passenger seat next to Tracy.

"Oh, can you drive a stick?" asked Adam.

"Of course I can drive a stick."

Adam made an impressed expression. "Sure, sorry. So, you're going to hold in the clutch and gun the engine a bit. Then when you're ready, crank the wheel and pop the clutch. Just make sure to keep the rpm's up and shift into second and stay there with your foot on the gas."

Tracy held the wheel and got a feel for the pedals then grabbed the ball at the end of the stick shift and looked at her passengers. "Ready?"

"Go for it!" said Mark.

Loni started the donut chant again.

Tracy turned and smiled at Adam. He was grinning ear to ear at her. She revved the engine, maybe a little too high. Everyone braced. She popped the clutch, and the car started to spin. The circles were a little reckless at first, but Tracy brought them under control, and they were back to doing donuts building a cloud of dust that engulfed them again.

Lonie was pressed against Mark as the bug spun around and around. She started holding onto his arm for support. Tracy took her foot off the gas and let the car's momentum spin them to a stop. She shut down the engine and they were all breathless with excitement.

"Oh, my God. I love donuts!" Tracy said with her hands still glued to the steering wheel.

"You did awesome. *You've* done this before," Adam kidded her.

"Yes, I'm a professional stunt driver in my spare time."

They smiled at each other.

"Hey, you guys want…" Adam started to ask Mark and Loni something, but he stopped when he saw them in a full-on make-out kiss in the back seat. He turned to Tracy and motioned with his head for them to get out of the car. She nodded in return.

They both hopped out and leaned against the warm

hood of the car next to one another while the cooling engine quietly rang with pings and knocks.

The dust had settled, leaving the night sky pristine and clear. They had ventured far beyond the glowing halo of town lights, allowing the stars to shimmer brilliantly against the dark canvas of the summer sky. A mere sliver of moon hung low in the heavens, casting a gentle glow over the landscape. The native saguaro cactus were silent sentinels, silhouetted and watchful over the entire desert. Their arms were twisted and bent, frozen in various poses that allowed your imagination to run wild with the reason why they grew in such a manner.

"So, ASU huh," said Adam breaking the comfortable silence.

"I guess."

They continued to watch the nightscape, doing their best to ignore the goings on in the back seat.

"Why NAU for you?"

"Have you been there?" he asked.

Tracy shook her head.

"It's in the mountains close to Sedona. I love that place. We used to go there when I was in the Indian

Guides, camping, and exploring."

"Indian Guides?"

Adam chuckled. "It's like Boy Scouts but from the YMCA." He looked at her with a smirk. "It's where the Jews go to experience scouting."

Tracy gave a little laugh. "Sounds cool."

"It actually was. I love going up to Sedona, so I'll be close. There is also skiing and other stuff there. Plus, NAU has a great physical therapy program."

"You want to be a physical therapist? That seems so random."

"Yeah, well, you get to be a doctor and don't have to deal with blood, guts, death. I hate all that stuff. I think I'd faint if handed a scalpel to do a surgery. I'm a total wuss at horror movies."

Tracy took a few seconds to process what Adam said, then, "You could be a baby doctor. Help create life."

"Yuck, gag me. Delivering babies is disgusting. Do you know how much goo comes out with the baby? I'd probably lose my lunch all over some poor kid as they come into the world."

Tracy was laughing and grossed out by the thought.

"Okay, I see your point. It is pretty gross when you

think about it."

"So, what about you? What are your life goals, Tracy Smith?" Adam asked in a mock adult voice.

Tracy let out a slow breath of air. "I need to get away from my mom."

Adam waited for her to elaborate while Tracy collected her thoughts on the subject.

"She wants me to become what she didn't. She has visions of me being a 'high society' woman someday. She manages a resort hotel and hobnobs with rich assholes all day. She dreams of being one of them, but of course they keep her at arm's length. She's always concerned with appearances and etiquette… hates my friends and of course, Joey." She looked up at the stars, then cringed and said, "She wants me to join a sorority."

Adam cocked his head as he considered this. "Never even thought about joining a fraternity. I don't think I could get in. They'd take one look at me and probably laugh."

"I don't think they'd laugh. You're super smart. They'd be lucky to have you."

"Well, what about you? You're smart. Everyone you meet likes you and you're super hot." Adam flushed with embarrassment after spilling that compliment and turned away. Tracy stared at him then smiled.

"We should both pledge. By this time next year, we could have a group of friends with names like Biff and Muffy."

"Right, we would be sporting cardigans, with our collars popped up."

They both smiled and looked up into the night sky for a moment without saying more. It was a cozy silence that lasted until Adam came up with a further idea.

"We really could become whoever we want to be. That's one of the reasons for going to college far away from home. It's a fresh start, a social do-over. Not that I don't love my friends, but I'm a little afraid of not accomplishing anything. For years I kind of thought we'd be the next Bon Jovi or Mötley Crüe, but…"

Tracy nodded her head. "You don't think you'd make it that far."

Adam looked at the outlines of the mountains in the distance. "Not a chance. You'll understand if you go to this battle of the bands."

"We only regret the things we never did, Adam." He gave her a look to express 'I don't know about that.'

Tracy socked him in the arm. "Well, maybe it will just be something to look back and laugh about fondly."

"Sure, what's funnier than public humiliation?"

"Nothing," she teased. "Come on, it will be fun. Loni and I will be in the front row doing this for you no matter what."

She held up her hand with the index and pinkie fingers up and the others folded down in the rock 'n' roll symbol, then pantomimed rocking out at a concert, head banging.

"Okay, okay. I'm in," laughed Adam.

Tracy put a hand on his leg affectionately. Adam looked at her and they had a moment, eyes locked. Tracy pulled her hand away before something more happened, like a kiss.

"Maybe we should call it a night before we have to hose those two off," Tracy said with a thumb pointing behind them to the back seat of the bug.

Adam slapped the hood of the car to get Mark and Loni's attention. "Hey, you two, come up for air."

Mark slowly raised his middle finger to them without a pause in the kissing.

"It's getting late, guys, let's motor."

"Come on, Loni, you don't want your brother to have to kill Mark on your first date," said Tracy.

Loni slowly pulled her lips from Mark's. "She's right. We should go."

Mark was heated up and visually disappointed. He saw Adam and Tracy standing at the window. "Adam, why don't you drive?"

"Sorry, dude, too stoned."

"Tracy?" Loni asked.

Tracy rolled her eyes. "Fine. I'll drive. But you two need to cool down. I don't want to look in the mirror and see some porno back there."

Loni looked up in horror. "Tracy!"

Adam and Tracy moved to get in the front seats, and she said quietly with sarcasm to Adam, "Like it's never happened." She chuckled off Adam's quizzical look.

Once they were all settled and Tracy had the engine idling, she said, "One more donut for the road?"

Everyone yelled 'Yes!' in unison.

The bug roared to life and performed a spinning donut then Tracy power-slid the car onto the dirt road leading back to town.

Adam and Tracy were waiting in the car, watching Mark and Loni finish saying their goodbyes on the front porch. The radio softly played while they sat there, and Tracy killed the engine after realizing the goodnight kiss could take a while.

"I remember meeting your mom a few years ago. She seemed pretty cool," Adam said breaking the silence.

"Oh, she's cool all right. She's still attractive, good job, hot young boyfriend who does everything for her. But as a mom? How she feels about her daughter…? On that subject she is the most disappointed woman in the world. If only she could have a daughter that dressed how she wanted, talked, walked, and thought how she wanted… It's almost like she would be happier with a doll rather than a daughter."

"I'm sure she just wants what is best for you. When your dad died in what, third grade? I remember people talking about how you guys would probably have to move away. How could your mom take care of you on her own and find work? But that didn't happen. She worked hard and you're still here. I know you want to follow your own path, and I get it, but it sounds like your mom just wants what is best for you. Maybe compromise with her in some way. Check out the sorority for yourself, then decide if you hate it or not."

Tracy listened without interrupting but Adam's whole siding with her mom completely annoyed her, by the time he finished she was pissed off.

"What the fuck do you know? She's a total bitch to me about everything. It's not just the sorority thing."

Adam realized that he hit a nerve and started backtracking. "Sorry, you're right. I don't know what I'm talking about. I shouldn't have…"

"Damn right! Just because you helped me with my homework doesn't mean you can give me life advice."

Tracy honked the horn to hurry Mark and Loni up.

Loni looked at the parked car with irritation. "What's her hurry?"

The front door suddenly opened, and Loni's brother Donny stepped out.

"All right, Tubbs, time for you and Crockett over there in the car to take a hike," he said.

Mark cringed at the latest *Miami Vice* reference he's had to endure this evening. "God, this was a bad wardrobe choice," he muttered to himself.

"Be nice, Donny. Bye, Marky. Call me tomorrow." She went in for a final kiss, but Donny got in between them and steered her into the house.

"There's been enough of that tonight," Donny remarked as he closed the door behind them.

Mark walked happily to the car and Adam opened the door to let him into the back seat. He flopped, lying down with his feet kicked up against the window.

"Cigarette?" Adam asked him while lighting one for himself.

"It almost sounds good, but it would take the taste of Loni off my lips."

Adam offered his to Tracy. She took it but her face wore a scowl. He lit another for himself. Adam took a long drag and stared out the window as Tracy drove. The Psychedelic Furs' song 'Heartbreak Beat' played on the radio while he watched the neighborhood streets go by along with any opportunity he might have had with Tracy.

There's a heartbreak beat
Playing all night long
Down on my street

And it feels like love
Got the radio on
And it's all that we need
There's a heartbreak beat

And it feels like love
There's a heartbreak beat
And it feels like love
I'm a heartbreak beat
Yeah, all night long

CHAPTER 12
Band Practice

In Freddy's cramped room, the Bellevue Boys were in the midst of rehearsing their latest original tune. The window shook with the reverberations of their crappy rock anthem, a cacophony of lyrics celebrating muscle cars and wild women, reaching a wailing crescendo. As the final chords faded into the air, Johnny, fueled by the adrenaline of the music, launched into a daring attempt at an airborne splits. His body soared with less than perfect form, falling way short of achieving a full leg extension.

"Dudes, that rocked," Johnny said then high fived each of them, though Mark looked disappointed.

"Adam, you were late three or four times, you too, Freddy. Johnny, you have to sing on key. We need to clean this song up. Can you guys just put some more effort into it?"

"What is your beef, dude? That was awesome," Johnny disagreed.

"He just wants to impress his new girlfriend, Loni," said Adam.

"Oh, yeah? You banging that?" Johnny asked with interest.

"Dude, it's none of your business. And I just don't want to embarrass myself on stage."

"I think you've fallen in love," Adam said in a mock sweet voice, hugging himself.

"Oooh, did she pop your cherry, lover boy?" Freddy piped in.

"I've told you; I've already had sex before."

"Right, with your cousin," chuckled Johnny.

"She wasn't my cousin!"

Freddy's little brother Daniel stood in the doorway. "Ug, you had sex with your cousin?"

"Get out of here, Daniel!" Freddy and Mark yelled out in unison.

Freddy threw a drumstick at his brother, and it hit the wall with a thud.

"Mom said you need to get your cars out of the driveway. The pieces of shit are leaking oil all over it!"

They all threw something at him, and he ran down the hallway to escape their wrath.

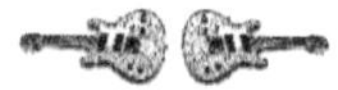

The boys finished moving their cars out onto the street. Freddy left his radio blasting from his car stereo; the bass was seriously pounding from the two subwoofers. The windows of the car were rolled down to rock the whole neighborhood with Freddy's headbanging playlist cassette. The boys gathered around his car to hang out.

"Dudes, listen to that bass. Those new subs thump,"

Freddy bragged.

"So sweet," agreed Adam.

Johnny turned toward Adam while he leaned against Freddy's car. "You going to bang Tracy?"

"I think I blew it with her last night."

"Johnny, do you know any other word besides bang?" Mark asked with disgust. He looked at Adam. "Doesn't it annoy you?"

"I barely notice what he says anymore."

Johnny scoffed, "What happened, did she find out you have a pussy like Mark?"

"Fuck off, Johnny," Mark said with a loud groan.

"I'm just kidding, dude. Don't have a cow."

Adam continued, ignoring the side show. "Everything was going great but then I agreed with her mom's point of view on something. She threw a hissy after that."

"Oh man, you should never agree with someone's parental units," Freddy schooled.

"I know… I was trying to be helpful."

"Helped yourself right out of some poontang," Johnny scoffed.

"Dude!" Adam and Mark exclaimed in unison.

Johnny laughed out loud to himself, loving that he finally got a rise out of Adam. The song on the stereo switched to a crunchingly loud Metallica hit. The side mirrors on Freddy's car violently pulsed with every bass tone. The boys started to play air guitar and toss their hair with each headbang as the song cranked up in tempo.

"Freddy! Turn off that noise!" Freddy's mom, Asami screamed from the window.

CHAPTER 13
Mommie's Little Girl

Tracy shuffled around her room in comfortable sweatpants, a loose-fitting T-shirt, and a terrycloth headband, methodically removing posters of rock bands, Harrison Ford, and Patrick Swayze from her walls. The room was a chaotic mess, with boxes, stuffed animals, and softball trophies scattered haphazardly around. As she worked, her mom rapped gently on the half-open door, announcing her presence.

"Hi, baby. What are you doing? Isn't it a little early to be packing?" She looked around at the bare walls. "You don't have to take all your stuff down."

Tracy looked up from her packing. "I don't want to come home from college one weekend and stay in some little girl's room that I don't know anymore."

Barbara stepped in and sat on the bed picking up a stuffed unicorn. "You're not throwing this stuff away, are you?"

"No, just packing it up. Ron said he would stack it in the attic for me."

Barbara looked around the room as Tracy packed away her belongings and memories into boxes. Nostalgia was rooted in every scrap of paper, every toy and knickknack. "I'm not sure I'm ready for your room to be empty. I was kind of hoping to come in and see all the things you loved whenever I got lonely. Whenever I was missing you…"

Tracy had a hard time looking at her mom. Barbara was beginning to tear up.

"I can't believe my little girl is going away to college. I still remember dropping you off at kindergarten. You were in a little pink and white dress that you hated so much, such a little tomboy back then."

"I remember all those dresses you would make me

wear. I just wanted to go to school in shorts so I could run around on the playground… play with the boys."

Barbara nodded her head, recalling. "The boys. It was always the rough and tumble ones you were drawn to. The troublemakers. The kind you'd see in…"

"Detention," Tracy finished.

They shared a smile for the first time in a long while.

"I'm sorry you feel like I'm a killjoy lately."

Tracy looked at her mom like, 'go on.'

"I guess I've been a little, controlling."

Tracy raised a brow. "A little?"

"It's just that I want the best for you. For you to have opportunities that I didn't, or that I missed out on."

"I know. I know," Tracy nodded. "It feels suffocating though to have someone try to constantly run your life."

"I'll back off some," Barbara told her, then gave a little smile, "just make a few suggestions is all."

Tracy melted a bit. "Okay." She approached her mom and gave her a hug.

They held for a moment, both feeling a moment of happiness and relief for the rare closeness they were sharing. Tracy was the first to let go of the embrace. She decided to throw another bone at her mom.

"There is this new guy. Completely against my type."

Barbara was shocked with interest. "Do tell. What's he like? Clean cut, jock, a football player?"

"Mom! Gag me, no." She got up and began to resume her packing. "He's short, Jewish… smart, funny."

She looked over at her mom to see that she was making a face. "He seems to agree with you on what I should be doing with my life."

"Well, that's one in the plus column. What happened to Joey?"

"We're still together, sort of."

"I think you should keep your options open, Tracy. You're going to meet so many nice guys in college. But I'm not trying to push. You'll make your own choices."

Tracy stared at her mom like they had just had a major breakthrough.

"See, I'm trying. Letting go, just a little bit," Barbara smiled and tossed Tracy the stuffed unicorn to put in the box.

CHAPTER 14
The Trash Can Game

While the TV displayed a drama filled episode of *Dallas*, Adam, Mandy, and their parents unwound after dinner. Lyle lounged in his La-Z-Boy, his hand resting on his burgeoning beer belly. Meanwhile, Adam sprawled over one arm of a cushioned chair, engrossed in the latest issue of *Rock Beat* magazine featuring Axl Rose on the cover. Annoyance flickered across his face as he read an article about the notorious frontman, the images stirring up memories of his disdain for Troy, the girlfriend-stealing poser.

Lyle got up from his chair when the show paused for a commercial break. He made his way to the fridge humming a country and western tune. He leaned in, scanning the contents of the shelves, but found nothing of interest and moved to the freezer compartment.

"I could totally use a scoop of ice cream. Anyone else want one?"

"Lyle, it's almost ten o'clock at night," Judy admonished him.

"Damn. What happened to all the ice cream?"

No one answered. He continued to look in the freezer, then the fridge and back to the freezer. "Damn it."

He closed the doors and grabbed his keys from a bowl near the kitchen. He struggled momentarily to get his boots on as the TV cycled through commercials. Once his boots were on, he headed to the front door. "I'll need to make it back before Carson."

After Lyle had left the house without so much as a goodbye, Adam slapped his magazine down on a side table and stood up.

"I'm going to my room."

"No loud music," his mom told him absently.

Adam closed his door behind him and grabbed his dumbbells. He stood in front of the mirror and began to do some curls. He cranked out six of them then dropped the bells on the carpeted floor with a muted thud. He did a quick bicep check at his reflection, flexing his arm muscles and revealing his small but defined bulge. He gave a satisfied smile to himself then turned toward his window that faced the backyard.

He was shocked to see the faces of Johnny and Freddy staring at him through his open window.

"Hey, stud," said Johnny with a smirk.

"Shit! What are you guys doing?" he said as he recovered from the shock.

"Johnny owes me five bucks. He bet me that you'd be jerking off," said Freddy.

"Give him another ten minutes," Johnny quipped.

"Why are you creepers at my window?"

"We're gonna play the trash can game. Figured you wouldn't want to miss it," Freddy said.

Adam gave the offer some quick consideration.

"Who's going?"

"Mark, Steven, Scott and Robert."

Adam looked at the clock, weighing the risk of sneaking out with his band mates and the three other neighborhood boys they grew up with then said, "Okay, let's go."

He grabbed a baseball cap and climbed out of his window to join the boys.

As the night cloaked the desert in its shadowy embrace, the group of boys rode toward their destination in silence. Steven and Scott navigated their bikes along the rugged trails that wove through the desolate landscape adjacent to their neighborhood. Tethered to the handlebars of their bicycles were hefty metal trash cans, clinking softly with each bump and jostle along the way. They pedaled in unison, their silhouettes cutting through the darkness, following the faint outline of the roadway. After a stretch of riding parallel to the street, they came to a halt beside a cluster of palo verde trees, their spindly branches reaching out like skeletal fingers against the starry sky. The brush, thick and tangled, flanked the deserted blacktop, stretching for miles in both directions, a silent witness to their nocturnal adventure.

They all came to a stop and surveyed the surroundings, deciding without discussion that this was the perfect spot to execute their fantastic prank on an unsuspecting driver.

They untied the cans and stashed their bikes out of sight from the road. Robert took a coil of rope from his backpack and set it on the ground. They dashed out of sight as the lights of a car emerged from the distance and they waited for it to pass.

"Steven and I lugged these things out here so someone else can set them up," Scott said, indicating the two trash cans. His white blond hair a moppish glow in the darkness.

"I'm way too stoned," announced Johnny.

"I'm not doing it. You guys are idiots and probably going to get someone killed," said Mark, folding his arms across his wide chest.

"Come on, Mark, we've done this fifty million times," responded Steven.

"Try three," corrected Mark.

Scott slapped Freddy and Adam on the back.

"Remember to set them further apart then last time."

"No doubt, that last car got totally banged up," Johnny reminded them.

Adam clapped his hands together and motioned for Freddy to follow him.

"Come on, Fred. Give me a hand."

They each picked up a trash can and started walking further down the road.

"Don't forget the rope," Steven said. He jogged to catch up and put the rope over Adam's head since he didn't have a free hand. They continued walking about fifty yards down the dirt shoulder before stopping and setting the cans down.

Adam looked back and noticed the other boys had crept out of sight. He and Freddy started to tie the rope to one of the trash cans.

"How much slack should we leave?" Freddy asked.

"I don't know."

Adam walked out about ten yards of rope and looked back at Freddy for approval.

"We don't want the trash cans to be too close to the road. That would look suspicious."

Adam walked out a few more feet.

"This should be good," he said. Car lights appeared down the road, and they waited by the side for a few passing cars that drove by without noticing them. They tied the rope around the second can and checked their work.

"All right, that should do it," Freddy said with a glint in his eye. "This is going to be amazing."

"Okay, let's wait until it's clear," Adam said.

Another car passed them, then there were no headlights in either direction. They nodded to each other and then carried the metal cans out into the open. They placed one on each side of the two-lane road with the rope stretching across the tarmac at about a two-and-a-half-foot height. The rope would be only visible to the driver if they were paying close attention and probably not until they were too close to stop in time from driving through the cord.

Freddy gave Adam the thumbs up. They booked it back over to where the others were hiding behind trees and bushes. They were mischievously laughing and giggling as they waited for a car to come down the road and into their childish trap.

"This is a mistake, guys. Somebody is going to get

hurt," warned Mark.

Robert scowled. "Shut up, Mark. Don't be such a pussy."

"No, this is wrong." Mark started to get up and do something about it, but headlights appeared on the road.

"Get down, dude!" Scott told Mark.

"Shit!" He ducked back down and watched as the lights got closer. He realized it was a truck as it neared. It was not slowing down and closing in fast. The driver didn't seem to have noticed the rope or the trash cans as they barreled closer and closer. "Shit, shit, shit," Mark repeated as the trap was about to be sprung. He shut his eyes at the last moment.

The truck hit the rope at about forty miles per hour. The rope went taut then yanked the trash cans from the sides of the road. They flew into the air as they whipped along, tethered to the speeding vehicle. Within seconds the truck grill was pulling the trash cans banging loudly behind it while attached to the rope. They flung in the air and bounced against the road sending sparks ignited from the collision of metal against asphalt. The cans made a huge racket as the driver started to swerve and fishtail the truck, hearing the noise and feeling the resistance of the added weight along with the firework display in his rearview mirror.

The brakes slammed, and the truck skidded to a stop in the middle of the street. The trash cans' momentum propelled them onward to crash into the vehicle's chrome rear bumper.

The boys were all staring in fascination at the scene. Big smiles lit their faces except for Mark's. Adam's smile quickly faded though as he took in the details of the scene.

"Oh shit," he said.

"What?" Freddy asked.

The driver's door of the pickup truck opened, and they saw the interior light illuminate the owner. Adam's dad stepped out of the truck with a look of pure rage.

"God damn it!" Lyle yelled out. He looked around the dark desert landscape erratically, then reached back into the truck and pulled out a shotgun from the gun rack mounted against the rear window. He slammed the door closed loudly with the twelve-gauge Mossberg 500 held tight in his clutches. He pumped a round into the chamber as he turned in a circle looking for a target for his fury.

"God damn it. You little bastards!" He was too far away to see the boys hiding off the side of the road in the darkened desert brush. He started yelling in all directions then fired the shotgun in the air, BLAM!

The loud blast pulled the boys out of their stupor. They raced to their bikes, stumbling and shoving each other out of the way. It was every man for himself as they unsteadily pedaled as fast as they could, crashing through the brush and cactus on their way, searching for the routes leading away from the scene of the prank gone wrong. One by one they found the correct paths and started riding through the desert back to their neighborhood on the narrow trails.

Adam and Mark were pedaling fast next to each other. They passed by Freddy and Johnny with Steven, Scott, and Robert riding out in front.

"Shit, shit! I've got to beat him home or I'm dead meat."

"He doesn't know it's us," Mark said breathlessly.

"Yeah, well if I'm not home when he gets there he sure as shit will!"

Freddy caught up as a fork in the familiar trail was on

the horizon. "The rest of us will head to Robert's house," he panted, riding fast.

They split up with only Adam taking the left route. He was riding as rapidly as he could through the desert terrain and then transitioned onto the neighborhood streets. He looked over his shoulder and he could see the lights of a single vehicle on the main road a short distance away.

A moment later he realized it was his dad's truck as it turned onto the street behind him. Adam tore into an alleyway to avoid the headlights and rode fast, skirting the roads.

Up ahead as he crossed a street, he spotted his dad's truck turning to approach his house. He watched the truck pass in front of him at a high rate of speed. Adam lifted off the seat as he pumped his legs harder. He jumped the curb passing behind his dad's Ford Ranger and rode to the alleyway behind his home. Skidding to a stop, he cut through the gate and stowed his bike back behind the shed then ran across the backyard toward the rear of his room. He hopped up and through the open window and hastily kicked his shoes off. He grabbed his guitar and put on a pair of headphones as he heard the front door slam.

Through his headphones Adam could hear his father hollering in the other room, "God damn little bastards!"

"What happened? What's wrong?" he heard his mom ask.

"God damn trash cans in the road!"

Lyle came thundering through the door of Adam's room. Adam looked up at his dad, feigning surprise. He lowered his headphones and set his guitar down, eyes full of mock of concern.

"What's wrong, Dad?"

"God damn trash cans in the middle of the street! I'm sure it was that degenerate friend of yours!" Lyle yelled at him with a pointed finger, his eyes full of rage.

"Who?"

"Freddy, that's who. Put two trash cans on the road with rope tied between them!"

"What? Shit, is the truck okay? Anyone hurt?"

"No, but I'm going to kick some little peckerwood's ass!"

"I'm sure it wasn't Freddy. He's probably at home," Adam said evenly, attempting to calm his fuming dad down. "I talked with him earlier. He was watching TV with his folks."

"I know it's something that little bastard would do," Lyle said shaking his head.

"Come on, you're always accusing my friends of this stuff. Let me call him and see if he's home."

Adam picked up the phone from the side table next to his bed. He dialed Freddy's house while his dad stood there scowling. He waited for someone to pick up the line and finally heard the phone being answered on the other end.

"Hey, man, what's up?"

Adam looked at his dad and shook his head to infer it wasn't Freddy outside tonight. "Just chillin' with your parental units? Me too." Adam listened and nodded his head a few times. "Oh yeah, I've watched that show too. No, not tonight. I've just been listening to music and playing guitar."

Adam kicked back on his bed and settled in to talk on the phone. Lyle's anger was deflating as there was no one to direct it at. He gritted his teeth, watching his son continue the phone conversation as if nothing happened. He then stomped out of the room unvindicated, slamming the door as Adam looked up to watch him leave.

Adam realized that the other person on the phone line said something he missed. "What?"

"I tell you I don't know what you talking about. Freddy not here, you idiot. How many times have to tell you!" Freddy's mom, Asami, said on the other end of the phone.

Adam breathed a sigh of relief as Asami hung up on him and the line went dead.

CHAPTER 15

Antonio's

Mark stood in the cramped confines of the bathroom at Antonio's Italian restaurant, fussing with the skinny black-tie snug against the collar of his freshly pressed, white button-down shirt. His long, unruly black curls had been tamed into a somewhat presentable style, awkwardly combed to one side, and tucked behind his ears.

As Mark wrestled with his tie, Scott backed through the narrow doorway. He was clad in faded jeans and a stained white apron layered over a Def Leppard concert T-shirt, a bucket of ice swinging casually in his grip. With a lopsided grin, he set the ice down with a muffled thud, his eyes dancing with amusement as he took in Mark's preoccupied appearance.

"Dude, you look ridiculous in a tie. I don't know why you wanted to transfer out of the kitchen to be a waiter."

"Tips. I need to make more money if I'm going to have a girlfriend. Six bucks an hour isn't going to cut it."

Scott's laughter echoed off the tiled walls of the restroom, punctuating his words. "You picked the wrong night to work for tips with Johnny cooking in the kitchen tonight." He gestured with a metal scoop, while casually shoveling ice into the urinals as if it were the most natural thing in the world. "Antonio's Italian shithole, where our specialty is pasta simmered in bong water, courtesy of Chef Johnny, the king of culinary arts." With a wry grin, he glanced down at the icy receptacles. "But hey, at least we've got classy bathrooms to make up for it, right?"

Mark rolled his eyes and finished with his tie. He turned to face Scott's approval. "Wish me luck, dude.

How do I look?"

Scott looked him up and down then raised one blond eyebrow. "Is your dick the special of the day or are you just showing off the appetizers?"

Mark looked at him quizzically. Scott motioned to Mark's unzipped zipper.

"Shit." Mark turned his back to him and zipped up.

Scott grabbed the bucket and slapped Mark on his shoulder blade with brotherly affection as he left. "Good luck tonight. I'll try to keep Johnny from jizzing on any of your orders."

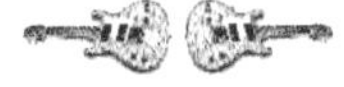

A light sheen of sweat covered Mark's forehead as he rushed around the bustling dining room. He finished writing down the dinner order of an elderly couple and frantically checked on the patrons dining in his section of the restaurant. One of his tables asked about the timing of their meal, concerned their wait time would be much longer.

"Let me check on that for you," Mark said and hurried through the swinging kitchen door that was adorned with a small porthole window to prevent collisions. Inside the bustling kitchen, Johnny was cooking amidst waves of wait staff, table bussers, and Scott, who was busy washing dishes.

"Johnny… is…" Mark flipped through his order book trying to find the right table's order, while having trouble reading his own illegible scrawl.

Johnny glanced up at Mark as he sautéed a breast of chicken in a mushroom and white wine sauce. "Use your words, Mark."

"Ahh, table seven is asking about their lasagna or is it linguine… shit, maybe…"

Johnny looked up at the tickets attached to the hanging clips above the stove's hood. "It's lasagna, dickhead, and it's been sitting under that heat lamp for five minutes."

"Okay, okay. I got it." Mark put the lasagna dish on his tray and started to go.

"Take the parmesan cheese or you'll be right back in here in thirty seconds," said Johnny.

Mark spun around almost crashing into a waitress and quickly plopped a bowl of grated cheese and a spoon onto his tray, spilling a large dusting of the parmesan onto the floor.

He was about to cruise through the swinging door when he spotted a family being seated in his section though the window of the door. His feet skidded to a halt as he recognized Loni and Donny about to sit down at a six top with their parents. Panic started to kick in and he stared, his body unwilling to go through the door. He moved quickly to the side, so his face wouldn't be seen in the window and a busboy with a tray of dirty dishes used his hip to slap open the door. It swung at Mark, and he flinched as the tray in his hand collided with the door sending its contents to squash into his chest.

"Sorry, dude! I didn't see you hiding there," said the busboy.

Mark slowly lowered the tray of food to find the top of the lasagna stuck to his new white shirt. The thick cheese and red sauce slowly fell away from the garment to slide down to the floor in a congealed mess.

Mark closed his eyes and muttered several curses to

himself as he heard Johnny and Scott laughing at him.

"You can't be hiding behind the dining room door, man," said the busboy as he moved on with his tray.

"Antonio is going to take that lasagna out of your pay," Johnny said then shook his head and showed a little pity for Mark. "Give me a few minutes and I'll have another ready. Why don't you take them some garlic bread while they wait?"

Mark set his tray down and grabbed a wet towel and tried to clean his shirt off but it was too late, the shirt was stained from the red sauce. He stood next to the swinging door peeking at the dining room.

Scott took the dirty plate of smashed lasagna off the discarded tray and watched Mark with curiosity. "What'cha looking at?" He moved next to Mark to peer out the window. Mark grabbed Scott's shirt to pull him back out of sight.

"It's Loni. She's here with her family! In my section," Mark said in a panic.

"No shit?" Johnny approached them and looked out the window.

"Johnny, don't let them see you," Mark said, pulling him back. The three of them were standing off to the side staring out into the dining room.

Antonio, the large, heavyset balding restaurant owner came out of his office to see his cook, dishwasher and newly promoted waiter crowded around the swinging door to his kitchen.

"What the fuck is going on here?" he said in his New Jersey accent.

The three boys turned, startled to find their boss hovering over them.

"Hey, Antonio," Scott said as he rushed back to his dish washing station.

Johnny turned and headed back to continue cooking leaving Mark stranded with the scowling owner.

"Um, just checking out the crowd, Antonio, looks like it's going to be a good night."

"Only if I don't fire you dipshits for standing around with your thumbs up your asses on my dime. Now get out there and take some orders before I send you back to washing dishes with your jerk-off friend."

"Sure, boss, I'm on it. Just going to plate some appetizers for one of my tables." Mark picked up his tray and started to add plates on top while nervously glancing at Antonio walking back to his office.

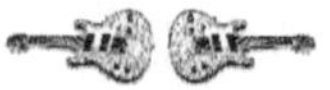

Loni's dad, Chuck, sat his broadly built frame into one of the seats at the table clothed in a red and white checkerboard-patterned plastic cover. His wife Beverly smoothed her dress as she eased into her chair, bracelets jangling as she scooted herself closer to the table. Donny kept his back ramrod straight as he arranged his silverware and napkin to perfect symmetry. Loni sat next to him and picked up her menu and started to look it over.

Mark glided into the room holding his tray filled with plates. He quickly dropped them off at several tables, watchful to see if Loni noticed him, but she was absorbed in the menu. Once his tray was empty, he approached with it held against his chest, attempting to cover up the massive sauce stain on his shirt. He did his best to play it cool as he arrived to stand at the head of the table.

"Good evening, can I start you folks off with something to drink?"

Beverly looked up from her menu. "I'll have a glass of white wine."

"I'll have a Bud," Chuck said without a glance at Mark.

"Make that two," Donny chimed in. He looked up from his menu and recognized Mark. "Oh wow! Gene Simmons is our waiter," he snidely remarked.

"Donny!" his mom scolded him.

Loni looked up with a surprised open mouth to see Mark standing there.

Mark offered her a shy smile. "Hi, Loni."

Loni took an almost audible gulp and glanced at her staring parents.

"Hi, Marky… Mark," she stuttered out.

"I didn't know you had a job, headbanger," said Donny.

Loni recovered from her shock. "Obviously, Donny."

"Just working here to earn some college money is all," said Mark.

"Well, I think that's great. Do you two know each other?" asked Beverly, as she looked from her daughter to the stocky teen standing uncomfortably at their table.

"Do they know each other…?" Donny started to say

with a chuckle before Loni elbowed him in his side to shut him up.

Chuck turned in his chair, now interested, and sized up Mark. "How do you know this boy, Loni?"

"We had some of the same classes in high school, some of the same friends, so we've a… hung out a bit," Mark piped in.

Chuck slowly turned his head to look at his daughter's avoiding eyes then back to Mark. "I wasn't asking you," he said slowly and deliberately, "I was asking my daughter."

Mark visibly shrank a bit, while his shoulders rose around his neck.

"It's like he said, Daddy, we know each other from school."

Chuck continued to stare at Mark.

"Well, tell the boy what you want to drink, Loni, so he can go and fetch it," Beverly said.

"Pepsi, I'll have a Pepsi."

Mark turned to go.

"With a cherry please," Loni called after him.

Chuck watched him go then turned to stare back at his daughter.

Loni looked up at her father's glaring eyes then back to her menu. He was still staring, and she looked up at him. "He's just a nice guy from school." She gave him a charming smile.

Donny chuckled and she elbowed him again.

"I can't believe they let these kids wear their hair like girls in these schools and at places of work. It's like the sixties all over again," Chuck said while shaking his head. He picked up his menu again to search for a dinner option. "You'd think his dad would hold him down and use a clipper to shave that head."

"Be nice to the boy when he comes back, dear. He's Loni's little friend," Beverly said.

"Mom, you know how much dad hates those headbangers, the last thing he'd ever want is for Loni to date one," Donny said with his eyes on Loni.

Loni gave Donny a quick angry look.

"Oh Donny, stop teasing her. That boy's not Loni's type." Beverly crossed herself. "No, no. your dad and I know just the guy for her."

Chuck looked up from his menu with a frown. "Bev, you're going to give away the surprise."

"I know, I know, I just can't keep a secret," she said

and threw up her hands with a conspiratorial smile on her lips.

Loni looked up at her parents, eyes darting to one then the other. "What secret? What's going on?"

"Your dad invited a guest to dinner tonight," Beverly said.

"What? Who?" She turned to Donny. "Did you know about this?"

Donny's head shook and he shrugged his shoulders.

Chuck looked up at a young man striding into the dining room. "Oh, there's the rascal now."

Loni looked up to see Craig Walker coming toward them. He wore a cat-that-ate-the-canary smile along with dark khaki pants, and a blue button-down polo shirt. His hair was a shade darker than milk chocolate and cut in a short stylish fashion. His jaw was square and his shoulders broad. There was a flash of white teeth as he approached with his arms open wide.

"There's the number one golfer at the club," Craig said with an enthusiastic finger pointing at Chuck.

A broad smile broke out on Chuck's face, and he returned the finger point toward Craig. "And there's the best caddie east of Pebble Beach." Chuck stood and shook hands with Craig, who then greeted the rest of the table.

"Mrs. G, you look lovely tonight. Hey, Donny." His eyes locked on to Loni for a moment. "Hi, Loni, you look fantastic."

Loni's face switched from surprise to a tight smile. "I didn't know you were having dinner with us, Craig."

"Oh, I owed him a dinner after his excellent guidance on the sixth hole the other day at the club," Chuck said with a dismissive wave of his hand. "Have a seat, my boy."

Craig smiled and seated himself next to Loni, who looked toward the kitchen window uncomfortably.

"So, how was Greek life your first year at UofA?" Donny asked the glowing, tanned Craig.

"Totally righteous! My frat brothers are the best. The house is a non-stop party." He looked over at the adults at the table. "But still keeping our grades up of course. We are all focused to the max on our education."

"Of course you are. All that hard work and dedication... got to blow off steam every once in a while." Chuck nodded his head and looked over at his wife for approval. Beverly returned his nod and smiled at him.

"Of course, dear. Boys will be boys."

"Right. Well, how about you, Loni? Your dad told me you're going to UofA too. Are you going to pledge a sorority?"

"I don't think Greek life is for me. I don't get along with too many girls and a whole house full of estrogen energy would just gag me."

Mark pushed his way through the swinging doors with his tray full of drinks, self-conscience of the now visible stain on his shirt. He was doing his best to balance the tray in front of him to cover most of the red and brown mess. He looked up when he arrived at Loni's table and his eyes went wide to see the good-looking young man now sitting next to Loni. He immediately recognized Craig Walker as one of the most popular guys to graduate from his high school. He stood there stunned as everyone turned to look at him.

"Um, is that my Pepsi?" Loni asked, trying to spur him out of his stupor.

Mark visibly shook it off. "Yes, cherry and all," he said picking up the glass of soda with a cherry floating on top of the ice cubes. He set the glass down with a bit of nervous shaking, then distributed the rest of the drinks.

"Whoa, looks like someone had a bit of an accident there," Donny said pointing at Mark's shirt. Mark slapped the empty tray against his chest in an attempt to cover up the stain. "I recommend eating with a bib next time, bro."

"That is quite a spooge you got there, man," chimed in Craig.

"Yeah, a little kitchen mishap is all."

Craig snapped his fingers as if he had a recollection. "I know you. You're Mike's younger brother, right?"

"You guys were on the baseball team together. He's going to UofA too," Mark answered.

"Yeah. Yeah, that's right. Your brother was a good ball player." Craig looked Mark up and down. "You never played, huh?"

"No, it wasn't my thing."

"What is your thing, dear?" Beverly asked him.

Mark looked over at Loni's mom and stuttered something out that sounded like 'aaggaahh.'

"Mark's in a band, Mom. He plays bass." Loni saved Mark from answering.

"Oh, how nice. A musician. I love the arts, the symphony is just magical," Beverly said enthusiastically.

"What kind of music do you play?" Chuck asked with a squint to his eyes.

"Metal mostly. You know, Crüe, Metallica, Maiden…" He saw the distaste growing on the faces of Beverly and Chuck. "Stuff like that, but I can play other things, like old folk stuff too."

Craig was watching Mark sink and decided to totally push him under. "Heavy metal, epic. Hey, I saw your brother on campus a few times, dude is totally losing his hair. I sure hope you don't follow in his footsteps, gonna make it hard to fit in with all those hair bands. Maybe you got a different dose from that Jew gene pool?" Craig nodded his head to Mark. "I'll be pulling for you, bro."

Donny gave a bit of a snorted laugh. "Me too, Simmons," he said, which elicited another elbow jab from Loni.

Mark stared daggers, then, "Can I get you a drink, frat boy?"

Craig smirked at him. "Beer."

"ID?"

Craig reached into his back pocket and removed his wallet. He made a show of flipping through a wad of twenty-dollar bills before handing over his driver's license.

Mark looked it over, noticing that the birthdate pegged him at twenty-two which he knew was fake since Craig would be the same age as his brother, merely twenty. He handed the license back.

"Looks like you must have been held back a couple of years. I'll be right back with your beer." He quickly turned and headed back to the kitchen.

Craig was unable to make a comeback in time and he saw Loni smile at Mark's jab.

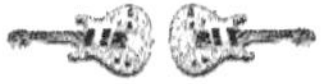

Mark entered the kitchen and set his tray down hard on one of the counter tops. Leaning over with his hands pressed down on the metal surface, he hung his head.

"What's got you trippin'?" Johnny asked, looking over at him while he was cooking.

"Craig frickin' Walker."

Scott shoved a tray full of dishes into the dishwasher. "That dude's here? With Loni?"

"Yeah, sitting right next to her like they are on a date or something."

"With her parents? What are they, engaged?"

Mark shot daggers at Johnny.

"Just asking. You don't go on a date with some chick and take her parents along unless you're proposing," Johnny said with a shoulder shrug.

"That dude is a player. If she's dating him, you've got no shot," said Scott.

"Thanks a lot, Scott."

"What is this, the Phil Donahue show?" Antonio yelled from his office doorway, staring at the boys conversing in the kitchen. They quickly picked up the pace of work and ended their discussion before the big man came out.

Loni pushed her half-eaten plate away from her as everyone finished their meals. Her dad gave a satisfied belch and patted his full stomach.

"You'll have to excuse my husband, Craig, seems the table manners he learned in the service were light on politeness."

Craig waved a dismissive hand. "My old man was an army guy, I know it's a sign of appreciation of a good meal."

"Right you are, Craig. Not going to finish your meal, Loni?"

Loni looked up to see Mark approaching the table. "No, I'm not that hungry, Daddy."

"You just don't want to stuff your face in front of Craig," chuckled Donny.

"As if."

Donny pantomimed shoving food into his mouth.

"Stop teasing your sister, Donny," Beverly scolded.

Mark arrived at the table, tray covering his shirt as he stood there. A young busboy started to clear the plates. "Can I get you all anything else?" Mark asked.

"Just the check," answered Chuck.

"Oh, can you get a box for this beautiful young lady?" Craig asked and stretched his arms out, putting one around Loni's chair with a smirking smile.

Mark narrowed his eyes at him. "I'll have your busboy take care of it."

Mark turned on his heels and strode away.

Craig raised his eyebrow. "Our waiter seems like he needs to take a chill pill or something."

"No doubt, guy's probably just jonesin' for his next score of dope," Donny remarked.

"Oh my, do you think he's a dope fiend?" Beverly asked, making a sign of the cross.

"Just look at him, total burnout," said Craig.

Loni aggressively moved Craig's arm from around her chair and shot up from the table. "He's not a druggy, you guys don't know what you're talking about. I'm going to wait in the car."

"Loni!" Beverly said in shock.

Loni stomped off toward the lobby of the restaurant. Craig stood up and said, "Shoot, I might have been a little harsh, let me go out to see if she's okay and apologize."

Craig hurried and caught up with Loni as she was walking out the door and put his arm around her just as Mark entered the dining room to see them exit.

Mark stopped in his tracks to see the front door close,

and Donny caught Mark's disheartened look.

"Yo, Dio, you got our check ready?" Donny said, raising his hand to Mark.

Mark let out a sigh and approached the table with the bill.

"Thanks for dining at Antonio's Italian eatery. We hope to see you again." Mark dropped the check in front of Chuck and slumped his way back toward the kitchen.

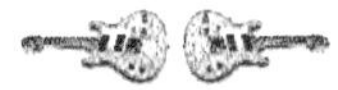

Loni shrugged off Craig's arm as she walked out to her family's car.

"Hey, what's your hurry? Are you, like, seeing that guy?" Craig asked, quickening his pace to catch up to her.

"No. Maybe. I don't know. What business is it of yours?" Loni made it to the car and yanked on the door handle, but it was locked. She turned and leaned against the vehicle with her arms crossed.

"None of my business really," Craig said, standing in

front of her. His eyes roamed her figure. "You really could do so much better, Loni. You're too much of a Betty to be dating some pudgy headbanger who's going nowhere fast."

Loni gave him a stern look. "You don't even know him. He's so sweet and kind to me with the most beautiful blue eyes…"

Craig laughed. "You make him sound like a puppy dog."

"Whatever."

Craig looked back at the entrance to the restaurant and decided that if he was going to make a move on her, now was the time.

"Look, you deserve a real man, someone with a future. You can't start your first year of college dating a loser." Craig gently moved a lock of bleached blonde hair from the side of her face. "Why don't I take you back to my place, let's get to know each other a little better. Hanging with me could totally boost your popularity around fraternity row…"

Loni smacked his hand away. "Drop dead, frat boy."

Craig loomed above her as his face clouded with anger and she stood defiantly in front of him.

Loni's family exited noisily, and Craig turned, a smile quickly thrown on to mask his scowling face.

"Everything all right out here?" Chuck asked as they approached the car.

"Totally. We were just saying goodnight. Thanks so much for dinner. We'll have to do this again sometime." Craig shook Chuck's hand in gratitude.

"You're such a dear, you need to come over to the house for a BBQ before school starts back up," Beverly said after kissing Craig's cheek. "Wouldn't that be nice Loni?"

"Awesome," Loni said dripping with sarcasm that went over her parents' heads.

"Then, let's make it happen," Chuck said.

"Just give me a ring a-ding-ding and I'll be there," Craig said with a smile while mimicking a phone with his fingers and hand. With a parting wave he made his way over to his new Corvette convertible and smoothly opened the door and slid in.

"Sweet ride, man," Donny called to him. Craig revved up the engine and with a backwards wave drove off.

"Cool dude, huh Loni?" Donny asked with a smirk.

"Whatever," she answered and tugged again on the locked car door. "Dad, can we go?"

CHAPTER 16
Fouled

The sun beat down on the cement driveway outside of Mark's house as the boys played basketball, clad in shorts and an assortment of T-shirts, some with the sleeves cut off. Freddy dribbled the ball while Mark guarded him, arms spread wide to block his view. Freddy kept an eye out for Johnny to get open, but Adam and Steven circled around, cutting off any potential pass.

"Watch him, Mark, don't let him shoot," Adam said.

Freddy faked a pass to Robert who was being guarded by Scott and then spun around Mark, leaving him in the dust to complete a perfect layup, dropping the ball into the basket.

"Shit, Mark! What the fuck?" Adam complained.

"Bite me, dude, you've been fucking riding me this whole game," said Mark pushing Adam away.

Adam stopped and looked down at his chest where Mark pushed him. "What was that for?"

"You cover him then." Mark picked up the ball and threw it about twenty percent too hard at Adam, who brought his hands up to catch it but jammed one of his fingers as the ball smacked into it.

The two boys exchanged furious looks.

"Dude!"

"Dude!"

Robert picked up the ball and rolled his eyes. "Oh great, a dude fight."

"What crawled up your ass today?" Adam aggressively asked Mark.

"I could ask you the same thing."

They stared at each other waiting for the other to break eye contact.

"You two pussies are just pathetic. You get dumped on last night by Loni and you just want to piss and moan all day, and Adam, you get dumped, twice, and just walk around whining like a little bitch. How many times have I told you, dump 'em before they dump you. Quit getting played and be the *player*," Johnny preached to them as the two boys squinted and furrowed their brows at each other.

Adam's face softened. "Loni dumped you?"

"She left with Craig Walker last night." Scott answered for Mark.

"Shit. Why didn't you tell me?"

Mark broke away from the staring contest and walked off to sit on the curb.

"She went to Antonio's with him last night," Scott continued.

"Yeah, and sat in his section, so he had to serve them food while the dude felt her up," Johnny added.

Mark shot Johnny a 'what the fuck' look.

"They were all over each other in front of you?" Adam asked.

Mark got up. "No. I don't know what he's talking about. They were there with Loni's parents and her dickhead brother. But I saw them leave together."

"Well, to be fair, you guys only went on one date. It's not like you were exclusive," said Steven.

Mark gave Steven a hard look.

"Well, it's true." Steven shrugged his shoulders and motioned for the ball. Robert tossed it to him, and the boys started shooting hoops in preference to continuing the game.

"You two need to pull your heads out of your asses and focus on the prize," Freddy said as his shot from the sidewalk swished into the basket.

Adam picked up the ball and hooked it into the backboard missing the rim. "What prize?"

"The battle of the bands."

"We need a second song for our set. The first one will be our new original so maybe we do a cover after," said Johnny.

"I like it. What about something from Mötley Crüe?"

"No, Kiss," said Mark brightening up a bit.

Freddy shook his head. "We should do Guns N' Roses."

"No Guns N' Roses!" Adam objected as an image of Troy popped into his head.

The boys tossed the ball around as they deliberated on the all-important topic.

"You should do something classic like from Maiden or Metallica," Steven suggested. Freddy and Adam liked that idea and said an enthusiastic 'yeah!' At the same time.

"Be real, you guys aren't good enough to play anything by them," Robert said dismissively.

"We've been practicing," said Johnny.

"I can't believe you guys even signed up for that. No offense," said Robert holding onto the ball and looking concerned at his younger neighborhood friends. Robert was twenty-two and lived in the house next to Mark. He had been kind of a loner in high school, preferring to hang out with the younger kids in the neighborhood. He became godlike to them when he was old enough to buy them beer. He relished the status his genuine legal ID bestowed upon him.

"We didn't sign up. We don't know how we got in," Mark said.

Steven looked at them quizzically. "Jessica signed you up." His words stopped everyone in their tracks. They all turned as one to stare at him.

"What!" Adam finally blurted out.

"I thought you knew. Troy told me. She knows one of the bouncers at the Gardens and he made it happen."

Adam put his hands on top of his head and started to pace. "Shit. This is payback. She must want to humiliate me."

Mark bent over like he was out of breath. "No shit Sherlock. And we get to go along for the ride all the way down into the frickin' gutter."

Adam sat down on the curb. Robert bounced the ball to Mark who caught it and then threw it hard at the backboard in frustration. He sat down next to Adam.

"You two need to chill out. What's the big deal? We always wanted to play a gig and now we have our chance," said Freddy.

"Yeah, you pussies are stressing about nothing. Freddy is okay on the drums, Mark is decent on bass, Adam can play by ear, and I'm the perfect frontman. We are gonna kick ass."

Adam looked at Johnny, then shook his head in frustration. "We only know five songs. Jesus, what was I thinking?"

"Just when everything was going so well. I'll never

have another chance with Loni after she hears us. And I'm sure she's still gonna go since Tracy will still be there to see Joey and his band."

Robert looked sadly at them, then in an attempt to cheer them up and rally the boys he said, "Come on, it won't be that bad. What songs can you guys play?"

Freddy counted the songs on his fingers. "We know 'Shout at the Devil', 'Back in Black', 'Dude Looks Like a Lady', 'Round and Round', and…"

"You can't let Jess win. You just have to play," Steven broke into the conversation.

They all sat or stood in silence for a moment. Adam made up his mind and got up, brushing himself off.

"Fuck it. Let's go rehearse."

He started walking across the street to Freddy's house. Johnny and Freddy looked at each other then started to follow him. Mark watched the three boys for a moment, then said "Fuck it," under his breath and made up his mind to join them.

Scott, Steven and Robert watched them enter Freddy's house. Scott picked up the ball and tossed it to Robert.

"This is going to be a fucking hilarious train wreck," Robert said, taking a shot at the basket.

"Definitely," the others agreed.

Adam pulled his car up in front of Jessica's house. He sat there, stewing, building up the nerve to confront her. He looked over at the front door then at the other cars parked on the street looking to see if Troy's car was present. He turned off the engine satisfied that the orange Camero was nowhere to be seen. He narrowed his eyes as he gazed at his reflection in the mirror and let out an angry breath. He grabbed the Oakley sunglasses that were on the passenger seat, opened the car door and climbed out. Swinging the door closed he accidentally dropped them on the pavement.

"Shit."

He swung his head side to side to see if anyone was watching then he quickly picked up the glasses. He inspected the lenses and noticed there was a visible scratch marring the tinted plastic.

"Whatever."

Adam popped the Oakley's onto the top of his head and walked up to the front door. He poked the doorbell three obnoxious times, then knocked for good measure. He casually leaned against the entrance way and waited for Jessica to answer the door after hearing her call out from inside the house that she was coming.

Hair in a ponytail, wearing white sweatpants and a cropped midriff revealing T-shirt, Jessica swung the door open and frowned to see Adam standing there.

"What do you want?"

"World peace, The Beatles to reunite, Elvis to be alive and my sister's stupid Guns N' Roses cassette."

"Those Troy's sunglasses?" she asked, nodding to the pair on his head.

Adam waggled both eyebrows and removed the sunglasses from his head. "Even exchange?"

"Hold on." Jessica closed the front door then came back a moment later with the cassette tape. "Here."

She held out the tape and Adam swapped her for it.

"I know about you entering us in the contest."

Jessica broke into a sly smile. "I was just trying to help you guys. Get you a gig."

"Bullshit."

They stared at each other for a hot minute.

"Are you guys gonna play?"

"Everyone at that party saw the flyer. That was probably your doing as well."

Jessica didn't answer but it was obvious that it was she who distributed the flyers on all the windshields.

"Well, we decided we're going to go for it."

She considered this, then shook her head. "You guys are going to make fools of yourselves. Look, I'm sorry. I shouldn't have entered your band without asking."

"It doesn't matter. I'm leaving in a week for NAU. Most of those people I'll never see again. Who's going to remember some dopey concert at the Tucson Gardens ten years from now?"

"I hope you're right." Her face softened some. "You're really leaving?"

Adam nodded his head and looked away from her, feeling a mist beginning to cloud his eyes as the weight of leaving home and all his friends wrapped around his insides.

Jessica moved just a bit closer to him. "I'm going to miss you…"

Adam shifted his eyes to meet Jessica's as she decided to move in for an embrace. She slipped her arms around his neck, and he found himself sliding his around the small of her back. He could smell the orange and peach notes of her White Shoulders perfume on her skin. They both eased their heads back to stare at one another, moisture gathering in their eyes. They were close to kissing and the temptation for Adam caused his heart to thud loudly in his ears.

He spotted a glimmer of self-satisfaction in Jessica's blue eyes, and it was like a slap that pulled him out of a fog. He pulled away and saw a pleasing spark of disappointment flash from her that became immediately hidden away.

As he stepped back, Adam realized that it was truly over for him and Jessica. They had been friends before they started dating, and while there was still a lingering fondness between them, it was overshadowed by resentment and the painful realization that their time together had come to an end. "You'd better be there at the concert. You started all this shit."

He turned and started walking back to his car, acutely aware of her gaze on his back. With his head held high and shoulders squared, he strode confidently, feeling taller than his five-foot-seven frame.

"I hope you've at least been practicing," she called out.

"Jess, I can play by ear," he replied, not bothering to turn around.

"I don't know if you can!" Jess hollered after him.

Adam got into his car and drove away, leaving Jessica to watch him go. She shook her head slightly, then looked down at the sunglasses in her hand. She held them up to the sunlight and spotted a large scratch on the lens.

"Mother fuc..." she muttered.

CHAPTER 17

Rock is Dead

Adam pulled up in front of his house to find his dad washing his truck in the driveway. Lyle took off his Wildcats baseball hat and wiped the sweat from his brow. He dropped his soapy rag into a bucket of murky water rimmed with suds.

"Hey, sport."

"Hey, Dad."

"I want to have a talk with you for a minute."

Adam stopped and looked at his dad with

trepidation. The trash can game he and his friends played a few nights ago flashed in his mind. His heart raced with worry that his dad had found evidence that he was involved in the dangerous prank that just so happened to randomly target his dad's truck.

"Okay," Adam responded with hesitation in his voice.

With crossed arms, Lyle looked down at Adam as he stood there squinting from the bright Arizona sun. "I know you've had a bit of strife this summer, breaking up with your girlfriend and all, but your mom and I really think it's best for you to stay the course and keep your plans to go to NAU."

"I know, Dad, but I'm not sure I'm ready to…"

Lyle held up his hand for Adam to stop. "I already sent in the tuition money, so you're going. Staying here with the influence of your group of friends isn't an option, so don't bring it up."

Adam held his tongue and looked past his dad, hoping to hide his mixture of anger and fear. He fooled himself that the moisture in his eyes was due to the sun's radiance.

"You know, I was hoping you'd choose the service

like I did. It would have instilled some discipline in you, but your mom didn't want that life for you, so I didn't push. You got yourself good grades which makes me believe you'll do fine in college, but you have some growing up to do and I don't think it can happen here."

Lyle paused his lecture and put his hand on Adam's shoulder. "Look, bud, you liked that place when we visited. You'll be just a short four-hour drive away. Set aside this indecision. This is for the best. Trust me, living away from home will make a man out of you."

Adam looked up at his dad, wanting to argue his case for staying. He wanted to claim that he and his friends had a real shot at making it as a rock band, that they were about to compete in a battle of the bands that could kick start them to stardom. On the tip of his tongue was also the thought he could go to school here in Tucson, live at home, but the words wouldn't come. The anger and obstinance drained from his body and he just nodded his acquiescence.

His dad stepped back proudly and looked at him with a glimmer of respect. "Good man. Think I could talk you into getting a haircut before school starts?"

Adam gave him a 'don't push it' look.

Lyle cracked a half smile. "Had to give it try, I was on a roll."

Adam started to make his way up the walkway.

"We all right?" Lyle asked.

Adam stopped and turned to his dad. "We're good. We're cool. Thanks for the talk, Dad." he headed toward the front door with Lyle watching him go.

Adam's sister, Mandy, sat cross-legged on the carpeted floor of her bedroom, lost in her music and focused on her sketch pad. Her headphones cushioned her ears, the world outside muted by the melodies that played on her Sony Walkman.

Adam arrived at her doorway, his eyes wandering over the room adorned with posters of Kirk Cameron, Rob Lowe, and John Taylor from Duran Duran. The corkboard caught his attention, filled with artistically drawn eyes and candid snapshots of Mandy with her girlfriends.

He gently knocked on the side of the open door. Mandy looked up, her concentration broken. After Seeing Adam, she pulled off her headphones and clicked the stop button on her Walkman, the room suddenly silent.

"Hey."

"Hey."

Adam came in and sat cross-legged next to her.

"What'cha doing?"

She picked up her sketchbook and showed him the drawing. "It's going to be a Buddha. I've been working on different religious idols and perspectives."

"Like any good Jewish girl would."

"Half Jew. Dad's not Jewish, he's… I forget."

"Yeah, well, nobody knows for sure what dad worships," Adam replied.

"I think it is some sort of TV deity," she quipped back.

Adam smiled at his sister's jab at their complicated father.

"I got you something," he said producing the Guns N' Roses cassette for her.

"Finally. How'd that go?"

"She's the one that entered us in that stupid concert."

"I heard."

They sat for a moment, then Adam picked up her sketch pad and flipped through the drawings, noticing her emerging talent.

"Did you decide if you're going away to college?"

"I think so. I'm pretty much committed now. Dad sent the tuition money in. Though Johnny thinks if we do well at the battle of the bands, we should all head to LA to get a record deal."

"Look, even if you guys were good, which you're not…" Adam gave her a hurt look, "hair band rock is dead. You just don't know it yet. You missed the window."

"What are you talking about? It's not dead."

Mandy shook her head at him in sympathy. "It's over. No one is going to care about hard rock, spandex pants, and big hair next year."

Adam stared at her like she had lost her mind.

"Here, listen to this. It's a bootleg copy from a band out of Seattle" She handed him the headphones and rewound the cassette that she was listening to on the

Walkman. She hit the play button and 'Smells Like Teen Spirit' by Nirvana played. The gritty but melodic guitar riff immediately set the stage for an energetic and rebellious introduction to the hard-hitting drum beat. The bass moved in to add depth and fullness to the overall sound. The vocals arrived with a rawness and intensity filled with angst and disillusionment. The cryptic lyrics captured a feeling of apathy and frustration as they blended from shouting tones into an almost bored inflection.

Load up on guns, bring your friends
It's fun to lose and to pretend
She's over-bored and self-assured
Oh no, I know a dirty word

Hello, hello, hello, how low
Hello, hello, hello, how low
Hello, hello, hello, how low
Hello, hello, hello

With the lights out, it's less dangerous
Here we are now, entertain us
I feel stupid and contagious
Here we are now, entertain us

A mulatto, an albino, a mosquito, my libido
Yeah, hey, yay

Mandy watched her brother as he was visibly entranced by the music that flowed from the headphones. She picked up a magazine clipping that had a picture of the band. They were dressed in clothing that looked like it came from thrift store racks. Their hair was unkempt and free from hairspray and dye jobs. Her brother eyed the image of the band members with thoughtfulness. He handed the headphones back to her after a minute of listening.

"It's good, but I don't know if these guys will be as big as Poison or Mötley Crüe."

Mandy looked at her brother with compassion. He had always been a little clueless and late to the party when it came to fashion sense and music tastes.

"Whatever. I just think going to college is a better choice for you. Besides, you can always take music courses as a minor to improve your guitar skills."

"Mandy, I play by ear," he responded with a confused look.

"Of course you do."

They continued to sit as Mandy went back to her drawing and Adam continued to look over the Nirvana photo and the cassette's hand written song titles. He focused on his sister, happy in her creative element.

"I'm going to miss you."

Mandy looked up at him, surprised by the rare display of brotherly sentiment. "Me too."

She gave him a sly smile. "But your room is going to make a great art studio."

CHAPTER 18

Quick as a Turtle

Mark slowly folded the white cloth napkins and placed the silverware on the tables before Antonio's Italian restaurant opened for business that evening. His work ethic was suffering from the rejection he had felt seeing Loni leave the building two nights ago with Craig Walker.

He shuffled around the table in his untucked white shirt that still showed a faded stain from the lasagna smashing against it. His mom had done her best this morning to try and scrub the sauce away but in the end, it was only marginally better after the washing.

The kitchen door was propped open, and Antonio glanced in to see his newest waiter moving at a snail's pace.

"Jesus, Mark! How can I afford to pay you by the hour when you set the table slower than a fucking turtle?"

"Sorry, Antonio, this is all new to me, remember," Mark said trying to squeeze a little sympathy from his boss.

"Setting the table is new for you? You must be the God damn apple of your mom's eye," he said with his hands on his oversized hips. "Speed it up, dipshit, or you'll be back to washing dishes before your shift is over."

Mark watched him walk past the doorway headed toward his office. Johnny appeared in the frame and pantomimed jacking off behind Antonio's back. He looked back at Mark, and they shared a chuckle.

Mark moved the tray stacked with silverware to the next table but set it perched precariously too close to the edge. He got halfway through the table setting when he accidentally knocked the tray to the floor, sending dozens of clean spoons, forks and knives clattering to the floor.

"Shit!" he cursed.

"Mark!" yelled Antonio from his office and he could hear him stomping toward the dining room.

Mark started to quickly pick up the mess when Antonio's large form filled the doorway.

"You need to clean those. At least you've had a lot of practice at that dishwasher," Antonio sneered at him.

They both turned at the sound of knocking on the front door of the restaurant. Antonio looked at his watch to see that they were still an hour from opening the door to patrons.

"Go answer the door. It must be a delivery. Tell them to bring whatever it is to the back. Think you can handle that, dipshit?"

"Yeah," said Mark resigned to take the abuse.

He walked over to the thick wooded door and disengaged the lock. He opened it with heavy irritation on his face which quickly turned to shock.

Loni stood there, the sun at her back casting a glowing halo around her golden hair. She wore short shorts and a white tube top, the light framing her in a warm, radiant silhouette.

Mark stood making some sort of sound like a cod fish gasping for air, his mouth half open as he stared at her. She cocked her head to one side, and he regained his composure and shut his mouth before he made any more incomprehensible noises.

"Hi, Marky."

"Loni, what are you doing here? We're not open yet."

She looked at him like he was a loon. "I'm not here

to eat, silly. I came to see you."

Mark was shell-shocked and didn't know how to respond. He chided himself as he let the moment linger far too long.

"Can I come in? I got you something," she said.

"Um, yeah, sure." He held the door open wider for her to enter. She stepped inside and looked around the dining room but stopped at the hostess counter. Mark finally noticed that she held a shopping bag in her hand.

She spun around to face him as he closed the heavy door.

"Marky, do you like me?"

His eyes widened as he was taken aback by her question. "Well, I... of course I do. You're awesome."

She nodded her head but there were traces of hurt feelings behind her eyes. "Then why didn't you call me yesterday?"

"I, I, I thought you were seeing that guy Craig Walker," he stuttered.

"What? If you thought I'm so awesome, why would you ever think I'd date a yuppie asshole like him?"

"Well, because you left here with him! I saw you."

Loni put her hands on her hips and stared at him sternly. "I did not leave with him, you dope. I left with my parents. He followed me out and I told him to bite it. I would never date a guy like him."

"I didn't know, I just saw what I saw."

"You should have called."

Mark hung his head. "I should have." He looked up at her. "I'm sorry, Loni. This is all my fault." Mark heard Johnny snickering in the kitchen, obviously listening in on their conversation.

Loni took a step toward him and put her arms around his neck. "That's okay, Marky. I forgive you. Just don't act like such a dope again, okay, baby?"

"Never."

She gave him a little kiss on the lips, leaving him wanting more.

She smiled at him. "Pick me up after work tonight? Buy me an ice cream?"

"Sure, baby."

She turned to go and looked back at him as she opened the door. "Your present is in the bag. Don't work too hard."

Mark watched her go then looked down at the shopping bag. He picked it up and looked inside. He pulled out a new, packaged, fresh white button-up shirt. His heart melted. He turned back toward the dining room with a goofy grin on his face. Antonio and Johnny were standing in the doorway, both slowly shaking their heads at him.

"Whipped," said Johnny.

"Totally," Antonio agreed, and they turned to go back to work but not before Antonio let out, "pathetic" under his breath.

Mark didn't care, he picked up the pace of his place setting and whistled a tune as he worked.

CHAPTER 19
Walk, Bitch

Tracy sat waiting on the front porch steps of her house reading the Steven King's thriller novel *The Dark Half*. She was losing track of the story as she was becoming irritated by the long wait. Joey was supposed to have picked her up twenty minutes ago.

It was her last day of work at a clothing store where she'd been a key holder for two years. She had never been late before but Ron had helped her sell her car a week ago so she could bank extra money for college. She figured she wouldn't need it since she would be living in the dorms on campus and could bus it home on the holidays.

She checked her watch again and blew out a breath of frustration.

The rumbling sound of Joey's Dodge Charger prompted her to shut the book and drop it in her bag. She stood up and walked toward the sidewalk as he parked in front of the house.

"You're late."

He kept his sunglasses shielding his eyes as his car idled noisily. He leaned over and popped the door open from the inside. Tracy dropped her bag on the floor and sat down in the passenger seat.

"It was swamped at the car wash," he said as an apology.

"If you couldn't take me to work, I could have asked Ron."

"Yeah, or your little lap dog, Adam," Joey said with a snicker.

Tracy just gave him a hard look and rummaged through her bag for some lipstick.

"I don't know why you had to sell your car anyway."

"I won't need it for college and this way I will have enough money to not work and just focus on school."

Joey drove a moment in silence before shaking his head as something bothered him. "Yeah, I guess you could ask a million different college pukes for rides up there," he said darkly.

Tracy turned toward him with an aggravated look on

her face. "What's your deal, Joey? Why can't you be supportive?"

"Supportive? How about you supporting me for once? You know, I work really fucking hard. And all you do is take me for granted. Joey, can you give me a ride here; Joey, can you take me and Loni there? Joey, how come we never go out to dinner? How come we never talk anymore? Jesus! Can't you see I'm just trying to make a life for us? I've got a lot on my plate if we are supposed to move in together at some point and you just magically expect me to drop everything and move my ass up to Phoenix so I can… I can what? Watch you go off to some shitty college classes with a bunch of geeks to get a stupid degree that you'll never use? What bullshit!"

Tracy stared at him like he had just turned into an alien from another planet.

"Joey, I don't know what the fuck you're talking about, but you need to walk back everything you just said."

"Fuck that," he said staring at the road while he drove, "you know that is all true."

"I can't believe you're laying all this on me right now! I'm going to be late for work because of you, on my last frickin' day. Then I'm leaving in a few days and you're having a full-on meltdown. What am I supposed to do with all this?" she yelled out in frustration.

"Don't go!" he yelled at her, then said more softly, "Don't go."

Tracy stared at him as he drove and realized this was hurting him too. The changes. She looked at him, wondering what their life would be like if they stayed together, if she didn't leave.

"Baby, I have to go…" she said, reaching out to put a hand on his arm. He abruptly stopped the car on the side of the road a few blocks away from her work at the clothing store.

"What are you doing?"

"Out. You should start getting used to walking everywhere, so walk, bitch," he said with malice, though unwilling to look at her.

Tracy was shocked. She held back the words she was dying to say at that moment and picked up her bag. She opened the door and slammed it shut when she was out. She stepped away as Joey peeled out, the back tires spinning, and his car sped away.

Tracy scooped a triple helping of ice cream into a large bowl, squirted a quarter can of whipped cream over the mounds and dumped a showering of colored sprinkles on top as she held the receiver of the phone to her ear with her shoulder.

Her makeup trickled down her cheek along with the wet tears as she filled Loni in on what happened with Joey.

"He told you to 'walk bitch'? He's such a dick, Trace," Loni said over the line. "Want me to have Donny kick his ass?"

Tracy shoved a spoonful of the frozen, sweet pain reliever into her mouth. "No… maybe. I don't know why he had to end it like that."

"Because he's a dick," Loni answered.

Tracy nodded her head even though Loni wouldn't see and scooped another helping into her mouth. She wiped her running nose and the ice cream from her lips with the sleeve of her sweatshirt.

"He ended it like that because he's a boy, an

immature, stupid boy," Barbara said as she stood in the doorway to the kitchen.

Tracy turned with a start at her mom's voice and noticed her mom had tears in her eyes as well. She had been listening to Tracy tell the story of her breakup with Joey and was completely crushed by the hurt her daughter had just suffered.

"My mom's here, Loni, I'm gonna go. Love you and I'll call you tomorrow,"

"Love you too, Trace. It will be okay."

Tracy unwound herself from the extra-long phone cord and hung the receiver back on the wall. She practically ran to her mom's nurturing arms and cried.

"It's okay, baby. I've got you. It's going to be okay," Barbara cooed to her daughter and stroked her hair for a few moments.

Tracy wiped her face and tears then stepped back. "I really don't even know why I'm crying. I've wanted to break up with him this whole summer. I just thought it would be more… copacetic."

"Of course you did, dear," she said moving a bit of hair from Tracy's face, "because you're a mature young woman. He is just barely more mature than a child. Most guys his age are." She paused and lifted Tracy's chin. "I should know, I've dated a hundred of them."

Tracy snorted a laugh and the two of them smiled at each other and laughed some more.

"Yeah, I know. What should I do now?"

"Go to college, kiss some more frogs… 'til you find your prince."

"Kiss more frogs?"

"Absolutely."

Barbara gave Tracy an encouraging smile.

"Thanks, Mom," Tracy said with another embrace of her mother.

Barbara glanced over at the bowl full of ice cream. "Is there any left so I can join you?"

Tracy laughed and went to the freezer to pull out the tub of ice cream and she and her mom finished it off and talked until the wee hours of the night about boys, school, work and music.

CHAPTER 20
Not Riding in the Vanagon

Adam drove up to Mark's house just as Mark and Freddy were loading Freddy's drums into Mark's mom's van. To his surprise, Loni, Tracy, and Cindy were also there, sitting in the shaded carport on folding chairs. The girls were chatting among themselves, barely glancing at Adam as he pulled in. Nervously, he checked his hair in the rearview mirror and gave his armpits a quick sniff to ensure he wasn't emitting any unpleasant body odor.

He tried to exit his car casually, aiming to look as cool as possible in his cutoff jean shorts and concert T-shirt.

As he opened the hatchback door to retrieve his guitar case, he accidentally banged it against the bumper and struggled to keep from dropping it. Unfazed, he slid on his Wayfarer sunglasses, closed the door with as much nonchalance as he could muster, and strode toward the van.

"Hey."

"S'up, dude?" asked Mark rhetorically.

"Nada."

"Put your gear in here," Freddy said.

Adam stuffed his guitar in with the other instruments and nodded over toward the carport where the girls were sitting and chatting quietly. "What's going on over there? Why are Loni and Tracy here?"

Mark smiled at him. "It was a big misunderstanding."

Adam raised an eyebrow. "Yeah? You guys are still…"

Mark nodded.

"Nice. I'm happy for you," Adam said and held his hand out for a fist bump which Mark gladly reciprocated.

"You should talk to Tracy," Freddy said.

Adam glanced over at the girls trying to get a read on Tracy, but she was wearing sunglasses as well and he couldn't tell if she had even noticed him at all.

"I'm not sure there's anything there."

"Nothing ventured, nothing gained," Mark schooled.

Freddy closed the van's rear door. "Hey, you guys thirsty?" he called over to the girls.

"Yeah, let's go grab some drinks at Freddy's house," Cindy said as she stood up, taking the hint to leave Tracy and Adam alone together. Loni quickly got up as well and the two girls headed over to Mark and Freddy.

"Want something, Trace?" Loni asked.

"I'm good."

The two couples headed across the street with their arms around each other happily. Adam slowly wandered nervously up the driveway toward where Tracy continued to lounge in the shade. He sat in one of the vacant chairs and took off his sunglasses.

"I left a couple of messages on your machine. I just wanted to say I'm sorry again."

Tracy moved her hair behind her ear and stretched out her bare legs, crossing them at the ankles. Adam did his best not to look too long at them.

"It's cool. I shouldn't have gone off on you like that. What you said was mostly true. I just didn't want to hear it. I think I've just been getting pissed off by people giving me advice that I know is good for me but annoys the hell out of me anyway."

"Yeah, I get it. I've had a dozen of those conversations the past couple of weeks."

"With your parents?"

Adam nodded. "Mmhmm, and my sister… and Mark, who by the way is a great guy and I'm glad that Loni is giving him a chance."

"He's sweet, which is not what she usually goes for… but is probably exactly what she needs," said Tracy.

Adam relaxed a bit, building up a little courage and then asked, "How are you and Joey?"

"Are you asking if we are still together?" she said, tilting her sunglasses down to show him her challenging eyes.

"No. Maybe."

"I'm going away to college in a week," she said as a non-answer. "You're going away as well, right?"

Adam looked over at Freddy's house where his friends were hanging out inside. The pain of leaving them behind, giving up on the band, rose in his chest.

"I am," he sighed, "just got to get through tonight."

She leaned forward and playfully punched his arm.

"When I said I'll be there cheering, I meant it. Loni and I will be the loudest."

Adam rubbed his arm and smiled at her. "That means a lot. Especially since you have no idea how bad we are."

"What songs are you going to do?"

"Well, we only have one original and then we have to decide which of the five covers we know to do after."

"What are they?"

Adam leaned back in the chair and counted the songs off with his fingers. As he was talking, Johnny drove up loudly on his black and red Ninja motorcycle. They saw instantly that he was already dressed for the stage. He parked and casually dismounted in his spandex pants, shirt with the sleeves cut off, headband, and bandanas adorning his body along with long dangling earrings. Mark, Freddy, Cindy and Loni emerged from across the street after hearing him drive up.

"Dudes, you're not even dressed yet. Come on, we got to bounce," Johnny said after sizing them all up.

"Chill," Mark told him. "We have a few hours. Plus, we have been loading everything into the van trying to make room for the four of us. Thanks a lot for your help by the way."

"You don't need to save space for me," Johnny answered.

"Why not, you're driving separately?" Freddy asked with genuine curiosity.

Johnny rolled his eyes and nodded toward the van. "I can't be seen riding in the Vanagon. I'll take my Ninja. Mötley Crüe always show up on their motorcycles for a gig."

"Whatever, dude," Mark dismissed him.

Loni planted a kiss on Mark's lips. "We'll see you there, baby. We have to go get ready too."

"Get a room," Freddy said.

Tracy turned to Adam. "You'll do fine. See you later," she told him without a kiss like Mark had got, but she shot him a wink as she sat down in Loni's car. It was better than nothing, Adam silently told himself.

CHAPTER 21

Makeup Montage

The sun dipped below the distant mountain range west of Tucson, casting an early evening glow over the late summer night. Monsoonal clouds draped around the peaks, reflecting hues of blushing pink and violet in the car windows parked in the paved parking lot of the Tucson Gardens. The building, a gray, industrial, flat-roofed structure with no apparent connection to its name, featured a marquee advertising 'Battle of the Bands' below its title, 'Tucson Gardens.'

A short line had formed outside the club, held up by

a long-haired bouncer in a sleeveless shirt that showcased his thickly muscled biceps. He flexed them needlessly while examining the IDs of the men and women waiting to enter.

Inside, two girls in miniskirts and heels sashayed past a couple of ogling young guys near a cigarette machine. The dark wooden bar was lightly attended at this early hour, with only a few dozen patrons scattered throughout the space. The stage to the left of the room commanded a large presence but was currently empty. Black drapes concealed the backstage area off the stage's left wing. Low tables surrounded the room, positioned behind a wooden rectangle of a dance floor that lay directly in front of the stage.

DJ Tarantula was spinning records in a raised booth in the far corner of the club. His long, dark, glossy hair hung in front of his face as he held a set of headphones to one ear. He fiddled with the tones of the sound system as he kept one eye on his work and the other on the waitress carrying pitchers of beer to the patrons. The song, 'No One Like You' by Scorpions, was nearing its end and he prepped the next vinyl record to start on the second turntable arranged in front of him.

"There's no one like you, my little rock monsters. I hope you're ready for a kick-ass time tonight. Dollar draft beer all night, just don't be cheapskates and not tip your waitresses. They're working hard for you," he said into the microphone that sat next to his mixing board. "The battle of the bands is starting soon so get ready for new up-'n'-coming headbangers to rock your world. 'Til then you got me, Tarantula, spinning the best metal on the planet. Now let's hear from the powerhouses of rock, AC/DC coming at you loud."

He expertly spun the track, 'For Those About to Rock,' sending it thundering through the oversized speakers hung throughout the room. The powerful anthem set the tone for the patrons, kick-starting their night of drinking and reveling.

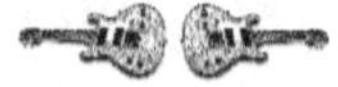

Adam slid into a pair of black leather pants and turned toward his mirrored closet door to admire how they hugged his form. Satisfied with the fit, he pulled on a sleeveless T-shirt, flexed his biceps in the mirror, and then picked up his dumbbells for a quick set. Feeling sufficiently pumped, he completed his look with a pair of rattlesnake skin cowboy boots and several bandanas tied around his legs and one against his forehead, locks of hair hanging over it.

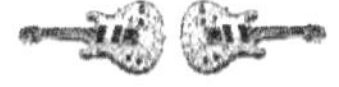

Mark laced up his high-tops as he sat in his desk chair wearing ripped-up jeans, a white dress shirt with the sleeves removed and a daring number of undone buttons left open to expose a sparsely haired chest. He stood up to gaze at the mirror hung upon the wall and mussed his hair to fall over this collar and gave himself an encouraging nod. He stuck out his tongue and waggled it in the mirror, stretching it as far out as he could. He then looked at his poster of Kiss in full makeup and costume, complete with platform shoes, and gave a pointed finger salute to his idol, Gene Simmons.

Freddy stood in front of the mirror in the bathroom he shared with his brother, an unlit cigarette hanging from his lip. He started to apply eyeliner and almost stabbed himself in the eyeball when a series of fast knocks at the door startled him.

"Freddy! Why my makeup scattered all over the place? You not let your dad know what you're doing, Freddy!" Asami yelled from behind the closed door.

"I saw him go in there with a handful of your makeup, Mom!" Daniel called out from somewhere else in the house.

"Freddy, why you want to look like girl?"

Freddy hung his head in frustration standing in the bathroom. "Jesus, Mom! I told you, I'm performing tonight! On stage. And the lights wash out your face. I have to wear a little makeup, just like actors in a theater or on TV, okay?"

"You so strange now. Need to stop hanging around strange friends. I don't know how you ever got girlfriend. Don't show her made up face, Freddy, or she leave you for 'nother guy who don't want to look like girl."

Freddy hung his head down, hands grasping the counter in a death grip. "Mom, I need to finish getting ready! This is my shot at being something great. Why can't you just support my dreams? The Bellevue Boys are playing a gig tonight!"

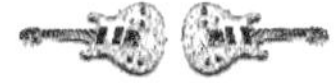

Loni and Tracy stood shoulder to shoulder in the small, brightly lit bathroom, each meticulously applying their eyeliner. The cramped space was filled with the anthem rock tunes of Bon Jovi blaring from a small boom box perched precariously on the edge of the counter. The rhythmic music seemed to pulse with the excitement of the night ahead.

Loni, her hand steady as a rock, leaned closer to the mirror. The dark eyeliner accentuated her almond-shaped eyes, adding a touch of mystery to her look. She wore a glittering silver skirt that shimmered with every movement, paired with strappy, black heels that gave her curvaceous frame a few extra inches. Her bleached hair was a voluminous masterpiece, teased, crimped and hair-sprayed to perfection, cascading down her back in vibrant textured lengths.

Beside her, Tracy deftly maneuvered her eyeliner brush, drawing a sleek cat-eye that complemented her playful smile. Her outfit, a tight red skirt and matching red heels, screamed confidence and allure. Her chestnut hair was painstakingly blown out to frame her face in a halo of glossy perfection calling to mind visions of Jacyln Smith from the *Charlie's Angels* television show. She gave her reflection a final, approving glance before turning to Loni with a grin.

"Ready to rock tonight?" she asked, her voice barely audible over the music.

Loni nodded, a mischievous sparkle in her eye. "Totally."

As they finished their final touches, the scent of their perfume mingled with the lingering hairspray, creating a heady concoction that filled the room. They gave each other one last once-over, ensuring every detail was perfect, from their perfectly painted nails to their meticulously styled hair.

The anticipation was palpable. With one final look in the mirror, they grabbed their tiny color-coordinated purses with metallic chain shoulder straps and headed out, the sound of their heels clicking against the tiled floor.

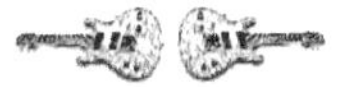

Johnny was cruising down the road under the darkening sky, the rumble of his motorcycle harmonizing with the distant sounds of the city. Neon lights flickered to life, casting vibrant hues of pink, blue and green across the asphalt, illuminating his path. His blond hair streamed behind him like a golden banner, caught in the wind as he accelerated through the streets of Tucson.

He was dressed in his stage outfit, and as the light faded, he refused to remove his mirrored aviator sunglasses. They were more than just eyewear; they were a statement, a crucial piece of the badass persona he had meticulously crafted for himself tonight. The reflective lenses caught the glint of passing streetlights, adding an enigmatic gleam to his already striking appearance.

He navigated through the maze of streets with ease, each turn and curve a testament to his intimate knowledge of the city's layout. In his mind's eye, he was a rock 'n' roll hero, an untamed spirit riding the waves of rebellion and freedom. His heart pounded with anticipation for the night ahead, the promise of his electrifying performance and adoring fans driving him forward.

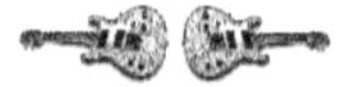

Mark drove the van with Freddy in the passenger seat to pull up to Adam's house. Mark honked the lame-sounding horn on the Vanagon to announce their arrival. Adam came out of the house decked in his rock costume and hurried to the van, opened the sliding side door and climbed into the seat behind Freddy. The van was packed tightly with Freddy's drum set and the two guitar cases for Mark's bass and Adam's Stratocaster alongside several boxes of amp cords and gear.

Synchronically, AC/DC's 'For Those About to Rock' was playing on the van's radio.

"Man, I can't believe we're really doing this!" Adam said.

"Be cool," warned Freddy.

"I am being cool. I'm just nervous. Anyone have a smoke?"

"Don't look at me," Mark said as he eased the van onto the main road.

"Are we gonna be late? What time is it?"

Freddy looked back at Adam. "Time for you to get a watch, and your own smokes."

Freddy pulled his pack of cigarettes out and handed one to Adam, then pushed in the cigarette lighter on the van's console. The boys rocked along to the AC/DC song, air guitaring and air drumming until the lighter popped and Freddy handed the little knob with the red-glowing metal coil to Adam. He lit the cigarette and inhaled a long drag, immediately feeling the refreshing jolt of nicotine to his nervous system.

Freddy returned the lighter to the dashboard and flipped down the sun visor to check his hair in the mirror.

"You have any hairspray stashed in this tin can, Mark?"

"Check the glove box."

Freddy looked in the glove box, but after finding

nothing he felt around underneath his seat until he came up with a can of Aqua Net.

"Aqua Net, score!"

Freddy fluffed his hair and then started to spray it heavily.

"Want some?" he asked Mark.

"Yeah, my hair is acting fucking weird tonight," Mark said after looking at himself in the rearview mirror.

Freddy handed the can to Mark who one-handedly mussed his curly locks and sprayed them into place while he drove and watched himself in the mirror.

Afterwards, he tossed the spray back to Adam who eagerly pressed the button on the large aerosol can, causing a thick cloud to develop in the van consisting of a dense mixture of cigarette smoke and sticky hairspray. All the while Adam's lit cigarette dangled from his lips.

"Dude, mellow out on that. You've got a God damn lit cigarette, and that shit is flammable!" Mark warned him.

Freddy looked back at Adam with an eye roll regarding the stressed-out Mark. Adam mimicked an explosion with his hands.

"It's no worse than smoking around one of your farts,

Mark."

"Ha, ha," Mark said, loaded with sarcasm.

Mark than leaned away from Freddy, pointing his rear end at him and let one rip.

"Fuck, dude!" Freddy yelled in protest while rolling down his window.

"Aw, man!" said Adam as the raunchy scent hit the back seat and he quickly cranked his window down as well.

Mark had a satisfied smile on his face as he continued driving. The wind coming through the windows was blowing the hair of his two best friends out of place as they gasped for fresh air.

CHAPTER 22

Headbangers' Ball

The parking lot of the Tucson Gardens was filled up with cars when Mark turned into the entrance. The boys looked at each other anxiously envisioning a packed crowd while Mark maneuvered the van to the back of the building where a separate rear door provided access to the backstage area. A heavyset Hispanic man with a shaved head holding a clipboard stood outside the open door.

The boys piled out of the van as the man approached

them.

"Who are you guys?"

"We're The Bellevue Boys." Freddy said proudly and opened the rear of the vehicle to start unloading the equipment.

"All right. Just the three of you?" he said looking at the notes on his clipboard and applying a check mark next to their band name.

"Uh, no, one more…" Freddy began as he turned his head toward the whine of a motorcycle's Japanese engine approaching.

Johnny rode up on his Ninja, swerving into the parking lot as cool as possible. He parked in front of them, no helmet, just sunglasses gracing his pursed-lipped face. He used his black leather boot that was adorned with barbed wire to engage the kickstand and dismounted the motorcycle like he was Wyatt Earp. He then shook out his long hair to fall gracefully around his face. He strutted up toward them and snapped his fingers in the air over his head, then with his hand still up, pointed his finger to the open side door. He arrogantly moved past them and entered the club without a word.

"Such a tool," Mark said under his breath.

The clipboard guy looked over at them, brow knotted in confusion.

"That's our lead singer," Freddy informed him.

"Whatever," the man said dismissively at the theatrics and walked away.

Adam shrugged his shoulders at Mark and Freddy then the boys began to unload the van and bring their instruments inside.

The backstage area was crowded with other musicians and their equipment. There was plenty of long hair, leather, spandex and attitude to go around. The boys started stacking their stuff along one brick wall with little to no help from Johnny who was smoking a joint and running over his lyrics to himself with hooded eyes.

Out of the corner of his eye Adam spotted Joey and his group hanging out a ways down the hallway. Joey saw him at the same moment and a smug smile formed on his lips.

"Oh look, everyone, it's the buttfuck boys," Joey snarkily called out to the small crowd of musicians, eliciting a few chuckles mostly from his own band members.

Adam gave Joey the middle finger before he could think twice about it. Joey's face darkened quickly. It was exactly the excuse he had been waiting for so that he could provoke the smaller Adam into a physical fight. He stormed toward Adam with his own band in tow.

"Wanna get your ass kicked, you little troll?" Joey said, pushing Adam in his chest then balling a fist to threaten him.

Something inside Adam gave him the courage to stand his ground. It wouldn't be the first fight he'd ever been in as growing up with Jewish heritage in a town that still clung to its western roots forced those differences to endure varying levels of bullying. He had long ago learned he could take a punch, as well as being quick and scrappy in a fight. Joey was an intimidating figure though, taller, a year older, muscled, and Adam knew he was no stranger to winning bouts at the Tire Tree, the common venue near their high school where disputes were settled with fists. It was a lone, leafless, dead tree that over the years had its limbs decorated with old tires from cars and bicycles.

Freddy, Mark, and Johnny hurried to his side to back

him up. The two groups stared daggers and swapped choice barbs with each other with only Mark trying to cool the situation down.

"Come on, guys, we are all just here to have a good time and play music," he pleaded.

"Shut up, fat ass!" shot back Joey with a heavy dose of venom.

Johnny aggressively shoved his way in front of the group and stabbed a finger into Joey's chest. "Don't be calling my friend fat, motherfucker, I'll kick your loser ass so hard you'll be picking your teeth up off the floor. We can find out just how tough you really aren't," he said coldly with murder in his eyes.

Mark looked over at Johnny at the surprise intensity on display at his defense. It was the first time Johnny had ever stood up for him and Mark was shocked to see it happen.

There was an enormous amount of harsh staring, and you could have heard a pin drop while both sides contemplated their next move. Freddy and the drummer for Joey's band stood comically wielding their drumsticks like weapons.

A bouncer the size of a grizzly bear, dressed like a

biker with rough tattoos that looked as though they were inked in a prison yard, shoved his way in between the two peacocking groups.

"Everyone better chill or you're all getting kicked out!" he warned them.

There were a few more seconds of the standoff before they all started to back down. Their fragile egos were all still intact as they mumbled about how their opposition was lucky the bouncer intervened.

"Why don't you guys leave this shit to that battle?" the bouncer said, pointing a thick finger at the stage.

Joey nodded his head at Adam. "You posers are gonna get creamed."

They all began moving back near their equipment, like it was their corner of a boxing ring, eyes still locked, unwilling to turn their backs on each other.

"You're the poser," Adam said once they were out of earshot.

"Not your best comeback," Mark said.

"I know. Shit. What should I have said?"

"Should have said something about doing his girlfriend," Johnny advised.

"Should have said something about his mom,"

Freddy added.

"Should have said something about *doing* his mom," finished Mark.

Adam looked at Mark with a 'what are you talking about' look.

"I really got nothing either. We're gonna get creamed anyway," said Mark.

The intervening bouncer pulled a piece of paper from his back pocket that contained a set list for the battle of the bands. He stared at it for a moment then looked at his watch.

"Where's The Rage? You're up first."

Joey looked over and raised his hand. "That's us."

The bouncer spoke loudly to be heard by all the band members crowding the backstage area. "Everyone gets two songs. Try to keep each of them to less than three minutes. We don't need any 'Stairway to Heaven' tonight."

Adam, on his tip toes, glanced over the shoulder of the bouncer at the list then back to his friends. "We're last. Let's go get a drink."

Adam, Mark, Johnny and Freddy settled into a table near the stage. A middle-aged waitress that looked like she slept in her car arrived to take their order.

"Hey, boys, sodas for you?" she asked dryly.

"Couple pitchers of Bud," Freddy replied, lowering his voice by an octave or two.

She looked at them with annoyance. "You have IDs?"

They all pulled out fake IDs. Adam's had a picture of a guy who was sporting a mustache, but looked close enough to be an older cousin, or maybe an uncle. The waitress glanced with a high degree of skepticism at his face.

"I shaved it. Old lady hated it."

The other guys presented IDs with varying degrees of forgery. She didn't totally buy any of them but let it slide because she really didn't care as long as they tipped and showed something resembling identification that they were of age to drink when she asked. With a heavy sigh she left to pour them their beers at the bar.

Adam looked up to see Loni and Tracy enter the club and his pulse raced. They both looked incredible dressed in miniskirts, high heels, big hair and lips painted with Revlon Cherries in the Snow lipstick. Adam swallowed hard as his mouth had suddenly gone dry. He met Tracy's eyes and she smiled at him, instantly melting him with a rush of blood to his head and… other places.

Loni hurried toward them with a finger to her lips to shush Adam as he was the only one at the table that noticed them. She surprised Mark by coming up behind him and clasping her hands over his mouth.

"Guess who."

"Mmmmm. Mmmmm," Mark incoherently mumbled.

Loni took her hands from his mouth so he could answer her, and she sat herself in his lap.

"The finest girl in the whole world. That's who," he said.

"Good answer, baby," Loni told him before locking her lips on his.

"You guys trying to make me Ralph before we go on?" said Johnny.

"You're just jealous," laughed Adam.

Adam and Freddy pulled up chairs for the two girls as they said their hellos. The waitress showed up with their pitchers of beer and a stack of cups. She didn't bother asking the girls for identification and moved on to wait on other patrons.

Loni glanced around the crowded club, checking out the guys and girls decked out in their most bitchin' rock attire. "It's like the frickin' headbangers' ball tonight."

"Have they started yet?" Tracy asked.

"Not yet. Your boyfriend is up first," Freddy said.

"Ex-boyfriend," Loni retorted.

Adam looked at Tracy to see if that was true.

"We broke up a couple of days ago."

"You didn't say anything," said Adam.

"Maybe it was none of your business," Loni said with a bit of a sing-song tone.

"It didn't end well, and I just needed some time," Tracy said.

A big group of their friends arrived at the club. Cindy, Jessica, Troy, Melissa, Ricky, Scott, Robert and Steven pulled over tables and chairs to join them.

Ricky gave Adam's hair a good mussing. "You ready little buddy?" he asked before sitting down.

"Watch the hair stoner," Adam said as he carefully put his locks back in place.

They started to pass around the pitchers of beer to pour for themselves. Troy held a pitcher, about to pour a cup for himself, but looked over at Adam for approval. Adam narrowed his eyes, then capitulated, and nodded that it was fine.

Jessica looked over at Adam sitting close to Tracy and had a hard time not showing a flash of jealousy and annoyance. She masked a smile and grabbed Troy's hand, bringing it up on top of the table to display in front of everyone.

"The axes are coming out, you little monsters!" announced DJ Tarantula. "It's time for the battle of the bands! Put your hands together for Tucson Gardens' native—The Rage!"

The crowd cheered as the lights went dim and several spotlights rotated, shining their bright lights onto the stage. Joey and his band burst into view with high energy. Joey was the lead guitarist, and he took his position near their singer out in the front. Their drummer sat behind the set of shiny black- and silver-colored drums and held his sticks aloft until the lead singer counted them down.

"One, two, one, two, three."

They started jamming with a loud metal sound that was similar to Metallica. The crowd was into them, especially a group of girls a few tables away. Joey wailed on the guitar with proficiency while he worked the female crowd in between licks and guitar riffs. He pointed, nodded and engaged as many girls as he could. He then turned his attention to Tracy with narrowed, combative eyes. It seemed like a silent, personal war was being waged between them.

"These guys rock," said Jessica while not taking her eyes off Joey and his guitar playing.

Joey moved his eyes from Tracy to Jessica, noticing her sitting a few chairs away. His eyes ogled Jessica's form as she turned her chair to face the stage. He let a little seductive smile form on his lips and blew her a little kiss. Jessica smiled and her face flushed with the attention. Joey gave Adam an FU smirk, while Troy was looking at Jessica with hurt and jealousy behind his eyes. Meanwhile, she was entranced with Joey's stage presence.

"I'm gonna get a pack of smokes," Adam said as he

stood up. He left toward the front lobby, fed up with the drama of the situation.

Mark had also observed the entire scene unfold, fully aware of what was going on. "He always smokes when he's nervous," he explained to the table.

"He looks like he's going to piss his pants," snarked Jessica.

"I'm sure he's gonna be fine. These guys aren't that great," Troy said.

Jessica shot Troy a look as if to say, 'shut the fuck up.'

Tracy had had enough of the theater as well. She got up after a moment and, straightening her skirt, left toward the entrance of the club where Adam had gone.

She peered around the lobby for a moment looking for him, but he was nowhere to be found. She decided he must have gone outside and exited the club to find him.

The night air had cooled from the sweltering heat of the day. The clear sky was showcasing a glimmering swath of stars. She glanced around the front parking lot packed with cars without spotting Adam, so she headed around the corner of the building and found him leaning against the hood of the Vanagon. He was nervously smoking a cigarette and fretting as she approached. Without a word she hit him in the arm playfully and leaned against the van alongside him.

Adam took another cigarette out of the pack and handed it to her, lighting it with his lighter. Tracy took a drag and looked up at the sparkling skyline.

"My mom was freaking out when I was packing. I thought she'd be happy to see me go. You know, getting away from Joey, moving on with my life and all."

Adam was uncertain of what to say. He didn't want to mess up again entering a conversation about her mom.

"I wish I'd been a little easier on her the last few years. I think I'm actually going to miss her and all her bogus advice." She paused for a beat. "Are you packed?"

"Just a couple of boxes full of clothes. Not sure if I'll even take my guitar."

"Come on. Don't let this contest get to you."

"I don't know if I'm going to be able to get up there. I really just pretend to play guitar. I only bought it because I thought it would help get girls."

"Come on."

Adam continued to fret and smoke his cigarette.

"I don't know if you noticed but I was a bit of a geek in high school."

Tracy couldn't stop herself from smirking at him.

"I don't think that's… quite true."

"Yeah, right. You look totally convincing. I was book-smart, short, and probably tried way too hard to fit in with the cool crowds. Me and all my friends did."

She gave him a 'stop it' look.

"Admit it. You thought so too."

Tracy looked at him, really seeing him, the vulnerability and earnestness, the sweetness. She dropped her smoke to the ground and took Adam's from his fingers and let it fall to the ground next to hers. His eyes moved from the smoldering cigarettes as she crushed them with her pumps, up to her bare ankles, legs, all the way to her heated eyes that were beginning to rip open his soul. She reached out and pulled him to her and they kissed passionately, the world falling away until only their embrace, pounding hearts and breath existed.

Joey and his band had a big finish to their set with a guitar solo that featured a fury of finger work by him ending with the pounding drums. As the music faded, Joey held his guitar in one hand over his head and flicked his pick out to the audience that was caught by Jessica while the cheers from the crowd filled the room. The Rage took their bows and exited the stage.

Jessica's eyes followed Joey as he disappeared behind the black curtains.

"Next up, put your hands together for Mother's Demons," DJ Tarantula announced over the speakers eliciting more cheers.

Loni slapped the table with excitement. "I heard these guys set fire to the stage a few weeks ago. Got them a record deal on the spot."

Everyone at the tables nodded in approval at that news.

Tracy and Adam slowly pulled away from their kiss. Adam opened his eyes to see Tracy opening hers as well. They gazed at each other, both surprised by how intoxicating that moment was.

"Wow. What was that for?" Adam whispered.

"Confidence," she lushly replied.

Adam nodded his head, breathless, feeling as if he was spinning.

"Yeah? I really do suck at guitar. I may need another dose."

He pulled her toward him, and they kissed again, this time, with the first kiss burnt into their memories, they came together again knowing each other's lips, tongue, and taste. The barriers of their hearts crumbled away between them.

Mother's Demons had set fire to one of their jackets. Two band members were trying to stamp it out as it burned in the middle of the wooden stage while the drummer and one of the guitar players continued jamming in front of the screaming and cheering crowd.

A young bartender with a fire extinguisher hopped up and slid across the bar like he was Bo Duke hood-sliding over the front end of the General Lee. He rushed up onto the stage and blasted the fiery jacket with a jet of monoammonium phosphate that coated the nearby band members in the yellowish powdery substance. The crowd roared with cheers and the bartender took a bow before jumping off the stage.

The song ended with the lead singer putting on the smoldering, ruined jacket and the band exited with hands raised in the rock 'n' roll symbol of raised index and pinkie fingers.

"God, these guys rock! Up next a band from all the way up in Phoenix, give it up for Strange Smells," DJ

Tarantula said over the sound system speakers.

The next band came on stage avoiding the remnants of the fire extinguisher. They had a Van Halen sound accompanied by a keyboard synth musician and were well received by the audience.

Mark was sitting with his arm around Loni's shoulder while the group around him was drinking and enjoying the show. He glanced over toward the entrance of the club wondering how Adam was faring and curious if he was with Tracy. He mentally had his fingers crossed that things would work out between them. He snuck a look at Loni's profile while she watched the performance. Mark couldn't believe his luck that this beautiful girl had taken a liking to him. He wanted to hold on to her with everything he had. His mind rolled around his plan to start watching what he was eating and spend more time on his hygiene. He inhaled the air around him to detect any failures of the deodorant he repeatedly applied this evening. He pursed his lips and nodded slightly to himself. 'All good,' he decided.

The waitress arrived with more pitchers of golden beer and set them on the table announcing, "I'm to tell you guys that you're up in two more acts."

Freddy sat up looking around the club. "Shit, where's Adam?"

"He better not have chickened out and split," said Johnny.

"I'm sure he's with Tracy," Loni said with a dismissive wave of her hand.

"Let's go find them," Mark said to Loni who looked forlornly at the excellent band playing on stage before sighing in agreement.

The two of them got up from the table and headed toward the lobby. The club was crowded now with headbangers and partygoers in every corner of the rooms. They weaved their way through the throng, holding hands, searching for Adam and Tracy. They ran into Joey sitting at the bar with two hot girls, well on his way to becoming drunk as a skunk. Loni pulled Mark to a stop in front of him.

"Joey, have you seen Tracy?"

"I've *seen* her, Loni, but I don't really give a shit where she is."

"Okay, well you don't have to be a dick about it," she scolded him.

"She's probably slumming it with that Jew boy, just

like you."

Loni took a drink from the bar and tossed it into Joey's lap. He leapt up, drenched in the alcohol and the other girls jumped back to avoid getting wet. Joey fumed with anger and looked ready to strike her across the face. Mark jumped in between them to protect her.

"Just try it," Mark said menacingly, fists clenched at his sides ready for a fight.

Joey hesitated and before he could recover his nerve the same bouncer from backstage arrived to keep the moment from escalating further. The big man stood looming behind Loni like a silverback gorilla.

"It looks like you peed your pants, Joey," Loni exclaimed and pointed at his soaked groin. He looked over at the two girls that were sitting next to him with embarrassment as they were staring at his wet spot while Loni laughed at him. Mark continued to scowl at him, standing at the ready alongside the large bouncer waiting for him to react.

"Fuck!" Joey said in exasperation and stomped off to the bathroom to dry himself off.

Adam and Tracy reluctantly broke off their kiss and came up for air. She kept her arms draped around his neck, their faces just inches apart. The adrenaline of the moment ebbed, clearing her mind. She gave Adam a comforting smile.

"This is just for tonight. You're leaving for NAU. Period. Understand?"

He pulled back slightly, taken aback, a pang of hurt rising in his heart.

"You and I are going to reinvent ourselves, remember?" she said softly.

Adam looked away momentarily before their eyes met again. Tracy removed her arms from around his neck and took his hands in hers.

"Then, later, two completely different people will meet again, become friends, and start something amazing."

Adam listened, letting her words sink in. It was not what he wanted to hear, but he began to understand.

His life had been full of indecision, too often he was too wishy-washy for his own good.

"A few minutes ago, I was thinking, I wish we would have gone out in high school, but now I'm glad we didn't." He paused for effect. "High school is over."

"High school is over," Tracy affirmed.

They looked at each other with the realization that they would stick to their decision and part ways… for now.

"So, what was that fifth song you guys know?"

Adam knitted his brow as he caught up to what she was asking, the question about what the second song in their set would be.

"Huh? Oh it's…"

Mark and Loni emerged from around the corner of the club.

"There you are! Dude, we got to go on!" Mark yelled toward them, waving for them to come back inside.

"Come on, it's almost time," Loni added.

"All right! We're coming," Adam yelled back. He gave Tracy a determined face, grabbed her hand and led her back toward the entrance to catch up to Loni and Mark.

CHAPTER 23

It's Only Rock 'n' Roll

The Bellevue Boys had their instruments ready to move onto the stage once the current performance was over. They didn't talk, or look too long at each other's faces—each of them was a bundle of nerves wrapped up in a vision of glam rock potential.

They stood amid the several musicians that had already performed along with the backstage manager and a couple of roadies, nodding their heads to music coming from the stage.

Mark stepped closer to the stage entrance to cheek

out the band rocking the house down. It was the only group that featured a chick as the lead singer. She was belting out rich, gravely vocals that elevated the enticing guitar riffs and chords that sounded straight from the airwaves of KLPX, Tucson's only local rock station.

Adam, Johnny and Freddy joined him to watch the end of the set. They all knew in their guts that this band was awesome, and their stomachs sank, thinking that they were going to have to follow these rockers' performance.

Adam stepped out even further to catch a glimpse of the audience. Most were on their feet, headbanging and singing along to the anthem-like lyrics. He could see Joey and his bandmates at the bar watching with salty looks on their faces as they could feel it too.

"I can't believe we have to go after these guys," Adam bemoaned as he walked back to his friends.

"They fucking rocked," Mark commented as the set ended and the crowd went wild.

"The Iron Siren, ladies and gentlemen. Up next are The Bellevue Boys, closing out tonight's battle of the bands," DJ Tarantula announced.

The Iron Siren exited the stage and passed by the boys

who were looking terrified. The singer stopped in front of Mark and fixed his hair, pulling curly locks to the front around his face. She than gave his check a soft slap and smiled at him.

"Don't worry, boys, it's only rock 'n' roll."

The Bellevue Boys watched her pass as she celebrated with her bandmates. The roadies pulled the previous band's drum set off and rolled Freddy's into the center toward the rear. With less than determined faces they took the stage. The bright lights were blinding, and Adam had difficulty picking his friends out in the crowd.

The floor in front of the stage was packed with standing room only. Adam spotted Loni, Tracy, and Cindy up front, their faces lit with hopeful smiles. As he made his way across the stage, his feet tangled in the cords that were snaking along the floor, but luckily he managed to stay upright. He thought he heard Joey snicker from the bar, though it could have been his imagination. Picking up the guitar plug, he attached it to his Stratocaster, causing a brief amplified buzz before it seated correctly.

He glanced over at Mark, who was already plugged

in and ready. Johnny stood with his head down, hands draped over the microphone secured to the stand, one foot tapping nervously. Freddy looked at Adam, seeking a sign that they were ready.

Adam could feel the silence growing uncomfortable, a pounding sensation pressing in from all sides—maybe it was just his blood thundering from his rapidly beating heart. He closed his eyes, took a deep breath, and then opened them to see Freddy poised with his drumsticks. Adam gave a quick nod.

Freddy smiled and clicked his sticks together over his head three times, then pounded the drums, launching into their original song, 'Highway Heartbreak.'

Adam hit the opening riff on time, a first in all their rehearsals. It was the cleanest, best performance they had ever played. On stage, they felt like they were born for this, as if they had been playing their instruments since birth. They relished the moments during the song when Adam and Mark rocked out side by side and back to back. At one point, Johnny threw his arm around Mark's shoulder while holding the mic, and they belted out the chorus together.

It was like magic happened that night… except for a

few mistakes; Freddy lost a drumstick briefly midway through, Johnny fumbled the mic stand, dislodging the mic, barely catching it before it came crashing to the floor, and Adam and Mark banged the necks of their guitars once, but in the end, they made it through.

The crowd's reaction was lukewarm, but their friends were overly generous with applause. To the boys, every clap sounded like thunder, every whistle a train blast. It was everything they had ever hoped for, and they looked at each other with wild eyes, exhilarated.

"Thank you, thank you," Johnny said as he stepped back up to the microphone.

Adam strutted up beside him to talk into the microphone. "We've got one more for you all. We're gonna need your help though."

"A lot of help!" Joey called out from the bar.

Adam shook off the jab. "Yeah, well, I think you all know this one."

Adam looked down at his hand holding the neck of his guitar and placed his fingers on the correct frets then looked at the other Bellevue Boys, making sure they were ready. He nodded at Johnny who took the microphone off the stand and walked in front of Freddy and his drum set.

"Kick it!" Johnny yelled.

They broke into a more than passable cover of the Beastie Boys' hit, 'Fight for Your Right.' This brought a loud cheer from the audience, who pretty much drowned out the boys' lyrics as they all knew the words.

You wake up late for school, man you don't want to go
You ask your mom, please? but she still says, no
You missed two classes, and no homework
But your teacher preaches class like you're some kind of jerk

You gotta fight for your right to party

Your pops caught you smoking, and he says, "No way"
That hypocrite smokes two packs a day
Man, living at home is such a drag
Now your mom threw away your best porno mag (busted)

You gotta fight for your right to party

For the first time the boys were on time, confident, and didn't miss a beat during the entire song. The vocals were traded between Johnny, Adam and Mark calling out the rap lyrics, mimicking the idiolect of each Beastie Boy they were emulating.

Tracy and Loni were in the front row rocking out, with Mark and Adam playing to them throughout the song. They changed the lyrics in the song to 'Ah mom, you're just jealous it's The Bellevue Boys'!

As the song ended, the audience was cheering and clapping for the boys. Johnny stripped off his sweat-soaked shirt and threw it into the crowd, which made a hole for it to land on the beer-soaked floor, uncaught and left there to remain unclaimed. Raising their instruments in the air The Bellevue Boys exited triumphantly from the stage.

The musicians and backstage crew gave them nods and high fives as they moved toward the rear door, Adam leading the way. He looked back at his grinning bandmates.

"That was awesome!" exclaimed Johnny slinging an arm around Mark in brotherly affection.

"They loved us," Freddy said holding a hand up for a high five from Adam, who gave it a solid slap.

"I need some air, man," Adam said leading them out the backstage door to the parking lot.

When they exited the back of the club Loni, Tracy and Cindy were there waiting for them to emerge. Everyone was charged up with excitement.

"Baby, you were so hot up there," Loni exclaimed, moving in close to embrace Mark.

"Yeah, dude, you were on fire," Johnny said with a hearty pat on Mark's back.

"You guys were great!" Tracy added enthusiastically.

"Really great!" echoed Cindy, planting a kiss on Freddy's lips.

"Do you think we have a shot at winning?" Freddy asked, pumped up by all the praise from the girls.

The girls quickly piped in their answers: "Doubt it." "Not a chance. No way."

The boys' faces quickly fell from the emotional high.

"Doesn't matter. You guys good?" Adam said then looked to his bandmates for an answer.

Freddy shrugged his shoulders. "Totally."

"Definitely," said Johnny.

"Fucking A," said Mark.

"Then let's blow this joint." Adam put an arm around Tracy and led them over to the Vanagon, opening the door so they all could pile in.

"Where to?" asked Mark as he slid into the driver's seat with Loni next to him.

They all looked at each other a little unsure about where to go next.

Loni's eyes brightened. "Donuts!"

"Donuts!" everyone exclaimed at once.

"What kind?" asked Adam.

Tracy gave him a quick kiss on the lips. "Both kinds."

"Let's do it," Adam said.

Mark started up the van and he turned up the radio as 'Sweet Child O' Mine' by Guns N' Roses played. They all joined in on singing the familiar lyrics as they cruised down the street away from the rock club. Adam even let it slide without a glimpse of Troy looking like Axl Rose entering his mind.

She's got a smile that it seems to me
Reminds me of childhood memories
Where everything was as fresh as the bright blue sky
Now and then when I see her face
She takes me away to that special place
And if I stared too long, I'd probably break down and cry

Woah, oh, oh

Sweet child o' mine
Woah, oh, oh, oh
Sweet love of mine

"Shit! My bike!" exclaimed Johnny.

"My drums!" said Freddy with a head slap.

"You guys are idiots." Mark rolled his eyes and flipped a U-turn, heading back to the club.

CHAPTER 24

California Dreamin'

The "Welcome to California" sign blurred past the faded blue Chevy Camaro, which was pulling an open-sided U-Haul trailer loaded with boxes, a set of drums, and a red-and-black Ninja motorcycle.

Freddy turned down the volume on the car stereo, the strains of the classic rock song 'L.A. Woman' by the Doors fading away, as he glanced over to see Johnny expertly rolling his fourth joint of the trip. Sunlight streamed through the dusty windshield, casting a warm glow on Johnny's concentrated expression.

"Those dweebs are going to be so jealous when we are playing at the Roxy one day."

Johnny finished his work and lit the stubby smoke and took a hit, blowing the streaming cloud out the open window.

"First thing we gotta do when we're set up is sell this piece of shit and my bike, get us a couple of Harleys."

"Dude, I need something to cart around my drums. And don't talk shit about my baby," Freddy added, patting the cracked dashboard.

"Just get a sidecar," Johnny joked, coughing up a little smoke from his lungs.

"How long do you think it will take us to land a couple of new band members?"

"Hmm, could take a bit. We need to be way more picky this time. Got to elevate." Johnny picked up a couple of cassette tapes from the floor. He looked over the album covers on the case and flipped them over, checking out all the images of the band members from the collection of rock 'n' roll tapes. He held out the case from 'Look What the Cat Dragged In' featuring the band members of Poison on the cover. "Check out these dudes… Mark and Adam were never going to cut it. You and I were the only ones holding up any standard of coolness and quality."

Freddy looked over at the cassette case Johnny was showing him while he kept the car and its trailer in the lane. Johnny handed him the joint and Freddy took a small hit before handing it back.

"Yeah, dude. We'll find some badass bros to join our group. A killer bassist and a guitarist that can actually play by ear," Freddy said with a knowing look at Johnny.

"Exactly," Johnny agreed, turning the volume back up on the stereo.

CHAPTER 25

Rock of Love

Mark balanced a plate full of prepared food that Scott had just finished plating with uncanny agility as he wove in and out of the kitchen and wait staff bustling through the restaurant.

"Good hands there, Mark," Scott said as he expertly tossed the food he was preparing in a sauté pan over a gas flame.

"You too, chef," Mark nodded as he used his hip to open the swinging kitchen door. He narrowly contorted his body to miss the new busboy as he entered the crowded dining room. He was feeling great after losing ten pounds in the last couple of months and building up some muscle by lifting the weights that Adam had left for him when he moved up to Flagstaff for college.

"Sorry, man," the frazzled busser apologized on his way into the kitchen.

"That's all right, you'll get it," Mark encouraged him.

He balanced the heavy tray in one hand when he reached a table of hungry patrons.

"All right, Mrs. Crane, you had the veal parmesan, and Mr. Crane you had the lasagna," Mark announced each plate to the guests as he set them in front of them. "Who needs a topping of parmesan cheese?" he asked and dished out the grated cheese from a bowl he had brought with him to the table.

He looked up at the porthole window in the kitchen door to see Antonio almost proudly smiling at him. He nodded at Antonio and then watched as he mouthed 'get back to work.' Mark shook his head and turned to look at his tables and thought about which one might need servicing.

His eyes caught Loni watching him from the hostess counter. She used her finger to tell him to come see her. He did a quick glance around finding nowhere he was urgently needed and then approached her.

She was wearing a hostess uniform that she had

altered to have the skirt many inches shorter than it was designed. She had also taken in the white button-up shirt so that it stretched provocatively over her breasts while also accenting her trim waist.

"Hey there, beautiful," Mark said arriving at her station.

"Hey there, handsome," Loni cooed and ran her finger over Mark's hair that was bound in a tight man bun. "You've been busy tonight."

Mark moved next to her and rested his elbows on the counter while they both looked out on the dining room.

"Yeah, place is rockin' tonight."

They both turned and smiled at each other.

"What if we had a place like this someday?" Loni asked with all seriousness.

"An Italian restaurant?"

"Yeah, you and me would be great at it."

Mark looked as though he was giving it a lot of consideration, then shook his head. "No. Not an Italian restaurant." He paused for effect. "We should open a donut shop!"

Loni squealed with excitement and threw her arms around Mark. "A rockin' donut shop!"

"Get back to work, you two!" Antonio yelled from the kitchen doorway.

CHAPTER 26
Way North of Tucson

A light carpet of snow covered the NAU campus, coating the buildings, walls, and trees in a soft blanket of glistening white flakes that twinkled brightly in the morning sun. The sidewalks, quad, and well-trafficked areas were a mess of dirty footprints as college students strolled between classrooms and labs, their breath visible in the chilly air.

Adam leaned against the red brick wall of the science building, writing in an open book. His face featured four-day-old scruff, and his dark brown hair, cut to one length, was touching his shoulders. To combat the cold weather, he wore a long-sleeved thermal under a T-shirt, topped with a wool-lined, second-hand jacket, giving him the look of someone who just stepped off a grunge rock album cover.

He finished his writing and closed the book, tucking it under his arm. Walking up the slushy, wet steps toward the entrance of the building, he paused at the top to check his watch. Just then, he felt a playful sock in the arm from behind.

He turned to smile at Tracy. She looked different now. Gone was the hot rocker chick from the summer. Her hair was in a ponytail, and she was dressed in tall, brown, soft leather boots over her denim jeans. A muted red jacket lay over her white button-up shirt and plaid scarf. They both looked older now, more mature in the way a semester at college could do to you. Tracy transferred to NAU to start the second half of their freshman year. January 1st rang in 1990 and they spent it together back in Tucson with their friends. There were a few tears shed leaving for the second time but less so than before, and it was getting easier to say goodbye.

"Trying to make us late for biology?" Adam asked,

raising an eyebrow.

"Don't get your panties in a knot," she retorted with a smirk.

"Come on, it's cold," he said, shivering for emphasis.

Adam put his arm around her shoulder, and they headed through the entrance to the science building. The warmth inside was a welcome relief from the biting cold outside.

"Yeah, you didn't tell me it was so cold here," she complained with mock anger, rubbing her gloved hands together.

"It's a lot hotter now that you're here," he said, raising both brows suggestively.

Tracy laughed and gave him another playful punch in the arm as they went through the door. The hallway was bustling with students, the hum of conversation and the clatter of footsteps filling the air. They wove through the crowd, making their way to the biology lab.

"Did you finish the reading?" Tracy asked, glancing up at him.

"Of course," Adam replied with a grin. "And I've got notes if you need them."

"Good," she said, rolling her eyes. "Because I totally

didn't."

They shared a laugh, their voices mingling in the warm air of the interior hallway as they walked together. They never did pledge to a fraternity or a sorority, nor did they ever make friends with a Biff or a Muffy, but they did grow up. They did reinvent themselves. They did find new friends and kept some old ones as well. Did they find in each other the love of their lives? Could it be considered lucky to have found that person at eighteen? Maybe for some, maybe not for others. Who could say what the future held for them in the new decade? What they did find though, was the courage to take a chance, the thrill of making a change, the strength to let go, and the fearlessness to step on a stage and bare their soul. And just like when Tracy told Adam, 'High school was over,' the two of them entered the biology classroom hand in hand, knowing so were the eighties.

A LITTLE MORE ABOUT ME BEFORE YOU GO

I graduated from high school in 1987 in Tucson, Arizona. It was a rad place to grow up—small, but not too small. I remember the population being about half a million Tucsonians spread out over an area of 250 miles. Tucson boasts a beautiful green desert landscape, nestled in a wide valley surrounded by mountain ranges.

If you're reading this and grew up with a mobile phone in your pocket, imagine a time when, to hang out with your friends, you actually had to go outside and find them. Sure, you could try calling their home number, but it might be busy or just ring endlessly because their parents didn't have an answering machine yet. It was a time when MTV played music videos exclusively, and Phil Donahue as well as game shows (think *The Price is Right* and *The Dating Game*) were the only reality television on your 19-inch TV. We spent a lot of time outdoors making up our own games, like the trash can game from this book. If your dad had a large wrench in his toolkit, you could be the hero of a hot summer day by cranking open a fire hydrant. It was an amazing time and place to be a kid.

Don't get me wrong, I would have loved to have a Dick Tracy watch, like an Apple Watch, but I would be a different person today. Speaking of today—I'm an entrepreneur and a writer of pirate stories. I've been on *Shark Tank*, produced a feature film, and have now published a rom-com novel set in the eighties. I live in San Diego with my beautiful wife, amazing daughter, and wonderful beach mutt, Roxy. I spend as much time as I can at the beach, swimming when the water's warm, surfing when the waves are clean and waist-high, and content with the fact my trestling days are behind me, glorious as they once were.

I hope you have enjoyed reading this book as much as I have writing it. If you'd like to keep up on my next projects, please sign up for my newsletter on my website and I'll include you in the 411. bryancantrell.com

You'll also find out more about me there, my other projects and passions. I also host a website dedicated to all things pirate, piratefanclub.com

It's a place for pirate history, merchandise, stories, and news.

I would be totally stoked if you would do an old headbanger a huge solid, please leave a review for *The Bellevue Boys* wherever you happened to acquire it. You know how much content thrives on reviews these days, so it would mean the world to me if you could share your thoughts on my '80s romcom book. I'd hate for it to end up forgotten in a bargain bin like the ones I used to see at Waldenbooks (RIP to the best bookstore of the '80s). Thanks for the support! With that said, later days, and better lays homies!